DINING FOR LOVE

Cover Design & Illustration: Melissa Doughty of Mel D. Designs www.melissadoughty.com

Editor: Katie Awdas, Spice Me Up Editing

ISBN 979-8-9888570-4-4

Published by Stafford Lane Publishing LLC

Author's Note

Dining for Love is an absolute romp of a novel. The angst is low, the giggles are high, and the on-page sex is, well, on the page. With handcuffs. Some may say you've been warned. I'll simply say you're welcome.

There is a bit of on-page action involving a gun and the dubious use of a cast-iron skillet. Any inaccurate portrayals of gun and skillet use are mine and mine alone.

Ready? Let's go!

CHAPTER 1

WILLA

I will not cry today.

The onions will not beat me.

I. Will. Win.

I do this every shift. I dice twenty onions, and somewhere around the ten-onion mark, things start to go sideways. Because that's when my nose starts itching, and instead of wiping it on my shoulder, I sniff to make it stop, and ka-blam, it's all she wrote.

Today is no different. Blinking rapidly, I fight the sting of impending tears from the mound of white onions piled to the right of the peppers. My eyes start to water—because I am *not* crying—but I persevere because we need more onions.

Lord knows that since it's Sunday, *and* summer, the diner will be packed to the rafters. Sundays always mean the rentals are full, but everyone got way too trashed on the first night of their beach vacation to actually cook the food they bought at the Piggly Wiggly yesterday. I can see it now: there will be a lot of headaches, a lot of coffee requested, and a lot of my famous Hangover Omelets ordered.

The secret, if you're wondering, is the Korean barbecue-flavored beef, plus, of course, a healthy amount of butter in the hash browns.

The bell over the door jingles, and in come my parents, Barbara and Dean Dash, the owners of Dash In Diner. Technically, they're also my employers, but we never let that get in the way. I've been working here in one way or another since I was ten. First, all they let me do was roll silverware at the counter after school, my legs swinging happily as I perched on a bright red stool and chatted with the customers. Then I was a dishwasher and a hostess, and once I turned sixteen, Dad finally allowed me to join him in the kitchen.

The minute I tied the apron around me and stood in front of the grill, that was it. I was a goner. I fell in love with the fast-paced rhythm of being a diner cook, the particular language between cooks and servers, the joy of doing something that makes people happy. Even after twelve years back here, that joy hasn't left.

"Where's Goldie?" My sister usually bounces in ahead of them with all the energy of a toddler instead of the twenty-six years she actually is.

"She won't be here," Dad answers good-naturedly. "Not feeling well."

"And the other two servers have called in sick," my mom adds with a roll of her eyes.

I smirk. "You mean hungover."

She shrugs and pours herself a cup of coffee, reaching for the sugar on autopilot. "Maybe, but it can't be helped. We need you out front."

The knife clatters to the cutting board. "No way." We all know I'm no good at it. Why would I subject anyone, myself included, to that kind of torture?

Dad chuckles and pats my shoulder, his hand strong and sure. "You're not that bad."

I gawk at him. "Dad. The last time I waited tables, I dropped an entire four-top's order!"

He doesn't bother with a response. Instead, he steps into his usual spot behind the grill and holds his hand out for my apron.

I sigh and untie it. "Fine. But I can't be held responsible for what happens."

"Willa Dean Dash," Mom chides, her honeyed voice sharpened with irritation, "You're perfectly skilled with more knives than I have names for, and you are a wizard in that kitchen. You could wait tables with one hand if you put your mind to it."

Yeah, that's…not true. But bless her for thinking it. The only place I'm steady is in the kitchen. Put me out front, and all bets are off.

Mom winks at me to soften the blow and begins the early morning routine: brewing more coffee, wiping down sticky menus, marrying the ketchup, and rolling the last bit of silverware. There's another ten minutes before opening at seven, and then we close at three.

I've told my parents that they'd make so much more money if they expanded their hours, but they won't do it. "Not worth our family's happiness," they say. And I guess I can't blame them there, because my twenty-eight years have been pretty great. Living in Lucky, Alabama, right on the Gulf Coast, might not be everyone's idea of heaven, but it is absolutely mine. There's nothing better than this small town and its people, even if they all get on my nerves every now and again.

Jake Daniels, our other line cook, swings in ahead of opening, muttering apologies and stepping into the kitchen without much fanfare. I'd rather *he* be out here waiting tables, but he adamantly refuses, and apparently, Mom and Dad listen to people when they're not family.

I look at dearly departed Granny's iron skillet, hanging on the wall over the coffee pot, and send it a prayer. I'm gonna need all the help today I can get. At seven o'clock on the dot,

Mom turns the sign to Open and the day gets going. She'll handle all the customers behind the counter and take everyone's payments, plus play hostess to the rest of the small diner. Together, we'll take care of everyone as best as we can and issue the requisite apologies for any slowness and thanks for patience.

Tom and Jerry lead the path into the diner like they always do, smiling and waving as they make their way to the end of the counter for their hours of gabbing and gossiping. They're the equivalent of those old guys in the theater box on the Muppet Show, except they're a lot nicer. More people trickle in behind them, and before too long, we're off and running another successful Sunday.

I'm doing pretty good and not messing things up too badly until late morning. Mom seats Chief Mac, Lucky's police chief, at a booth instead of his usual spot at the counter. He's got someone with him, and when I finally get a chance to turn around and say hello, I screech to a halt.

Because the man with Chief Mac might be the most gorgeous human I have ever laid my eyes on. Thick, wavy dark hair and tan skin that looks way too good beneath the white T-shirt he wears. A T-shirt that seems to be clinging onto the man's biceps for dear life, and honestly? I might be jealous of that shirt.

"Um. H-hi."

"Hi." He smiles, and I blink rapidly, trying furiously not to pass out. Because holy bright smile and dimples, Batman. Is this legal?

My hands shake a little as I grab for the notepad in my server apron, but it tumbles out of my hand, the green and white pages fluttering as it flops on the ground.

Of course this happens. Why wouldn't it?

Muttering to myself, and absolutely certain that Hottie McDimples is watching, I bend to grab the pad.

Except I'm me, so instead of it being this graceful bend-and-swoop thing like Elle Woods, I whack my head on the edge of the booth's Formica table.

"Ow," I whine, dropping my pen and reaching up to touch my throbbing forehead. That's definitely going to leave a mark. And if, by some miracle, my head isn't sporting a massive bruise, the sheer mortification of this encounter will be certain to haunt me for a thousand lifetimes.

"Willa Dean, you okay?" Chief Mac's voice is full of concern.

Groaning as I grab the notepad, I slowly bring myself back to standing. "It's just Willa, Chief, and yes, I'm...fine." I try to throw him a smile, but it's probably more like a grimace based on the way his eyes widen and his head jerks back a bit.

Hottie McHotPants slides out of the booth, and *whoa*. He's tall. Not overwhelmingly so, but still. Tall. And broad. Oh God, that's a lot of chest. *Breathe.* And now he's bringing his hand up to inspect me for injuries, and sweet baby Jesus, could he just...not?

I reel away from his raised fingers and repeat, "I'm fine," while gesturing for him to sit back down.

He does no such thing. In fact, the man steps right into my personal space. "You really did a number on yourself," he murmurs softly. He smells like laundry detergent and some kind of cedary spice, and even his breath is minty.

Then I look up to meet his eyes, and I swear on a stack of blueberry pancakes, my knees literally weaken. They're a gorgeous deep green, framed by thick black lashes, and they're laser-focused on me, and for the love of all that is holy, I really, really need him to stop.

"Coffee? Tea? Water?" I blurt the words without thinking.

He smiles again, and the bit of scruff on his face isn't enough to hide dimples so deep I could swim in them. Good lord, this isn't fair. It's impossible to focus with the way his eyes are... eyeing. Is that a thing? It should be. He's a walking crime. Come to think of it, Chief Mac should arrest him.

"Coffee, please," he says, sliding back into the booth and handing me my dropped pen.

In through the nose, out through the mouth. In, out. In, out. I take the pen and scribble the order down with shaky fingers, along with a note to get Chief the same.

I breathe my way back to the coffee pots, and hallelujah, I don't pour the coffee all over myself as I get their orders. When I return, I'm no less dazzled by the man, and it's beginning to be a problem.

"Guess I should make the introductions," Chief says, nodding at Hottie. "This is my nephew, Reid MacKinnon. Reid's gonna fill in for Jessica while she's on leave with the new baby. Came all the way from Miami." Chief's chest puffs with obvious pride while I keep a smile pasted on my face, trying desperately to reconcile the fact that I'll be forced to look at this man on the regular for the next three months.

Look, and of course not touch, because a man like him—sophisticated, flawless, and clearly put-together even in a freaking T-shirt and jeans—would never go for a woman like me. I may love being a diner cook, but it's not the classiest of jobs. Come to think of it, most men don't go for me, period. It's the one drawback of growing up in a small town: I know way too much about the guys around here, and I don't even show up on their radar.

It's all for the best. I smell like fried food most of the time, anyway.

"Reid, this is Willa Dean Dash."

Seriously with the Willa Dean. I increase the wattage on my smile, and it makes my head throb where I hit it. "Just Willa, Chief." The only people still allowed to call me Willa Dean are my parents, and even that's dubious on the best days. Which today is not. Not even remotely. Today is a day I'd like to rewind and stay in bed with the covers thrown up over my head.

Maybe permanently.

Reid flashes another blinding smile. "Nice to meet you, Just Willa."

Oh, and he's got jokes. Great. "Any food?" I croak.

Chief orders his usual, and then it's Dimples McGee's turn. He consults the menu far too long before finally shutting it with a snap. "Two eggs, over medium, wheat toast, dry, and bacon, extra crispy."

I manage to write it all down before whirling on my heel to flee. Mom catches my eye as I pass her.

"He's cute," she singsongs.

Yes, he's cute. He's also so far out of my league, it's not even funny. My sister, on the other hand? "Goldie's type, for sure."

CHAPTER 2

REID

I S THIS REALLY happening? Every pair of eyes have locked on me in the past five minutes, even the ones that look like they belong to tourists. Less than twelve hours in town and I'm already the center of attention in this small town diner.

It's...unnerving, to say the least.

But I can handle it. I've spent eight years in the Miami Police Department, three of those undercover, so what's a little staring? Besides, these people are far less intimidating than the scum I'm used to. The diner itself is cozy, decked out in retro red booths and black and white Formica floors. An honest to goodness jukebox is nestled in one corner, and a yellowing Coca Cola clock hangs on the wall behind the counter. I get the sense that the place has been around a long time, and while it's clear there are modern updates, the hat tip to nostalgia is alive and well. I take a sip of coffee and turn my attention back to the grinning man opposite me.

"Good, huh?"

I raise an eyebrow. "It's no Cuban coffee, Uncle Jack."

He chuckles, then points a finger at me. "Watch your tone, young man. And it's Chief Mac around here."

"Got 'em all fooled, huh?" I joke.

"Exactly." Then he crosses his arms and leans across the table, all traces of humor aside. "You sure you're safe here?"

I scoff. "Perfectly. With the arrests we made thanks to my undercover work, the Bunnies are on the run."

"You were *shot*." His voice is full of pain when he says it, as though he was the one who took the bullet.

I shrug it off. "It's a scratch, and it could have been a lot worse. You, of all people, know it's a hazard of the job."

He levels his gaze on me. "Let me rephrase this. You were shot when you were found out."

Okay, fine. He's got me there. I shift in the booth, trying to find a spot that isn't too lumpy. "Listen, Chief Muñoz knew I needed a break, and what better place than a little town on the coast of Alabama? Charming, by the way."

Jack harrumphs with a smile, letting me off the hook like always. "It looks charming, but we've still got our share of crime, Reid. No drug cartels like what you're used to dealing with in Miami, thank goodness, but it's not exactly a leisurely stroll every day on the job."

The waitress, Willa, brings us our food, and I flash another smile at her. I can't help the little bit of harmless flirting. She blushes furiously, and it's stupidly satisfying. In Miami, guys like me are a dime a dozen, and no one gives me a second glance.

Willa's cute. Natural. Nothing like most of the women I'm surrounded by back home. She wears no makeup, and her long dark hair is pulled up in a messy ponytail with too-long bangs falling into her eyes. Her clothes are worn and appear way past their prime. The overall effect is of a woman comfortable in her own skin—most of the time. Right now, she can't look at me without turning multiple shades of red, and I'm far too pleased by it. She leaves, as flustered as the two other times, and I turn my attention to breakfast. It's good. Solid food that's easy to do, but there's something extra in it that tells me it's made with care.

After a few minutes, another person approaches the table. There's no stopping the cataloging my brain does on autopilot: male, late twenties, trim build, glasses, neatly trimmed beard, no visible tattoos.

"Chief Mac, good to see you." The man turns a friendly glance at me. "And who's this?"

"Reid, Matty. Matty, Reid," Uncle Jack grunts, then goes back to shoveling hash browns in his mouth. Clearly the man is a fan of the food, as well.

I hold my hand out for a shake. "Nice to meet you."

"You, too," Matty responds. "You look like a...wait, don't tell me."

I glance at Jack, who stays focused on his breakfast. I'd be suspicious if it weren't for the way his mouth twitches.

Matty snaps his fingers and points at me. "Got it! Horses."

I lower my fork. "What?"

"Goats, then. Definitely a hooved animal." Matty crosses his arms and studies me. "Llamas?"

I eye him. "Respectfully, what the hell are you talking about?"

He laughs, completely at ease with what feels like an incredibly insane conversation. "I'm a veterinarian. I can usually tell what kind of animal a person likes within seconds. You seem like a horse person."

It takes me a minute, but then I start laughing. What kind of town have I found myself in? Even better, what kind of *people* have I surrounded myself with? "I'm from Miami, my friend. No horses for me."

He narrows his eyes. "No goats, either?"

"Definitely no goats." I pick up my fork.

He snaps and points. "Ah. Rabbits."

I grimace as Jack hoots across the table. "Goats before rabbits."

Matty looks thoughtful. "Okay, well, I have time to sort you out."

I hold my hands up. "No pets. I'm only here for three months." After I explain the situation, using the storyline we've discussed—I'm in town on a break and covering for Jessica while I'm at it—Matty grins.

"Police dog it is."

"You're relentless." But I have to smile. This guy is just as charming as the rest of the town, if a little pushy.

After breakfast, I follow Jack to my new place, a fully-furnished two-bedroom with more space than I know what to do with, and a massive backyard and fire pit just begging for me to sit out there with my guitar. And bonus: The price is ridiculously low. I scan the property, noting the places I'll need to install security cameras. I may only be here for three months, and I'm certain I'm out of the Bunnies' range and off their radar, but I'm not stupid. Lucky for me, the owner was thrilled with my request for a three-month lease, and he was even more delighted when he found out I was a cop. I got the feeling he was used to the standard week-long vacation renters.

"Great place," I tell Jack. "Thank you for everything."

He pulls me into a hug and slaps my back a little harder than necessary. "Anything for my brother's baby boy."

I groan. "Keep it up and I'll tell him about all the times you let me drink Mountain Dew when I was a toddler."

His eyes are bright with mirth. "You would never."

"Try me, old man," I retort with a wink.

Laughing, he jerks his thumb to my truck. "Let's get you settled."

It doesn't take much. The only things I brought were clothes, so it takes all of five minutes before my bags are sitting in the middle of the living room floor, a pile of black amidst the ocean-side chic that decorates the room.

"That's it?" Jack eyes my paltry set of possessions.

"I'm only here for three months, *Chief Mac*." I make sure to emphasize the name.

He exhales, the movement making his graying mustache puff out. It's a rare man that can truly pull off a mustache—I don't care what the college kids are doing these days—and Uncle Jack is up there with Magnum, PI. Dude can flex the facial hair. "Wish you'd stay longer, kiddo."

My chest squeezes at the affection. "You know I'm not cut out for the small-town life, Uncle Jack. I need the bright lights and the glitz. Does this place have any good dance clubs?"

He makes a face. "Do you even know how to dance?"

"Who says I'm going to clubs to dance?" When his expression gets even more sour, I hoot with laughter. "I'm *kidding*, Uncle Jack."

He grunts. "Maybe you are, maybe you're not. But I'll tell you, this place has a way of working its way into your heart. I'll ask you to stay again in a month."

Yeah, I doubt that. But I don't argue as I walk him to the door. "See you for my first shift tomorrow, Chief."

LATER THAT AFTERNOON, AFTER RUNNING SOME DUE diligence on the houses surrounding me—like I said, I may be temporary, but I'm not stupid—I've cracked open a beer and have made friends with one of the Adirondack chairs in the backyard. The house behind me has a couple in it, no kids, and a yippy Schnauzer named Mr. Tink. The one on the left has a retired couple and no visible pets. To my right is a two-story with only a widow in it; her daughter Betty is the station's receptionist and general office manager. Something tells me I'll meet the woman before too long. There's a smaller, one-story place behind the main house, too; I think it's called an in-law suite or something like that. Carriage house? I don't know what it's called. "Small house" works. It's closer to where I sit in the backyard than to the bigger house that Betty's mother is in. No records on a tenant, but based on the grass pattern leading to and from it, someone definitely lives there.

I'm on beer number two and have pulled out my guitar when the tenant herself shows up, and it's the waitress from this morning. Willa. I stop strumming, figuring she'll see me and at least say hello, but she blazes right past, the twenty yards of distance enough to make me invisible.

She opens her door and walks right in. The light goes on, and two seconds later, she's visible through the open kitchen window once more.

Oh.

She's a little *more* than visible, because she's in the process of removing her shirt. I watch as she peels it off to reveal a black bra, and then she takes her pants off. I can't *see* that part, but the motions she's going through make it pretty obvious.

Suddenly, she turns her head and meets my gaze through the window. She freezes as I smile and hold a hand up in greeting, then she ducks, and I hear a muffled yelp. A few seconds later, the light goes out.

Laughing to myself, I lean for my beer and take a deep swallow. If half-naked neighbors are part of the scenery, maybe it won't be so bad around here, after all.

CHAPTER 3

WILLA

I SLAM THE masher into the potatoes like a mad woman.

This entire town is obsessed, and I hate every second of it. Every customer for the past three days is all Officer Reid this and Officer Reid that, and come *on* already. Can they just let it go?

No. No, they cannot.

Which means he stays in my head, as well. I can't shake thoughts of him. The way his muscles filled out that T-shirt. The way he smiled. The way he looked at me.

Ugh.

And it's pointless. Someone like that won't ever go for someone like me, and I'm flat-out pissed at myself for even thinking about him. There's no use to it, so why, *why*, can't I get him out of my head?

My potato mashing gets more and more insistent until Dad says he thinks I'm going to pull a muscle. "It's food, Dad. It's not like I'm deadlifting weights over here."

Dad snorts and flips the burgers on the grill behind me.

Over at the counter, Tom raises his coffee, and Goldie moves smoothly to pour him some. "Have you seen our new officer yet, Goldie?"

Goldie shakes her head. "Sorry to say that I haven't, Tom. More for you, Jerry?"

I keep my eyes on my work, grabbing a handful of cheddar cheese to fold into the mix.

"Thanks, Goldie," comes Jerry's voice. "What are we calling him? Officer Hubba-Hubba?"

I roll my eyes.

"Officer Mac?" offers Goldie.

"Not to be confused with Chief Mac," Tom says.

I tune them out. I can't believe the guy is my new neighbor. Worse: He saw me practically *naked*, in my absolute *worst* underwear. Not that I even really have good underwear, but still. These were the very worst.

The only bright spot is that he's here for a short time. I won't be facing an entire lifetime of mortification. Just…three months.

Three very, *very* long months.

"Order in!" Goldie calls out and lays the new ticket in the window, then swivels away to continue working.

I grab the order. "Chicken club, grilled cheese, drop two fries."

Dad repeats it back to me, and I shove the ticket into the wheeled holder above the window.

The amount of hijinks I have pulled in these last few days to hide from Reid is absolutely ridiculous. Yes: Hide. Because, of course, he's been sprinting out of the house to go on a run when I've been trying to leave to open up the diner, leaving me to do a one-eighty to crouch behind Agatha's car in the driveway. And, okay, maybe it's fine to see him when I'm totally clothed, but I'm not great at making small talk. Especially when the person I'm supposed to be talking to is brain-meltingly hot and my stupid self can't help but get all giddy every time I see him, like I'm a pitiful grade schooler.

And then, when I come home at night, there he is, not even

fifty feet from me, sipping on a beer like some…some *person* enjoying their backyard. Forcing me to speed walk past him with my face buried in my phone, pretending I don't see him or hear him, when all I want to do is get inside and shower to get the diner smell off me immediately. Only now I've got to make sure the blinds are closed before stripping in my house like a normal human being.

Honestly, the least the man could do is be ugly. Is that too much to ask?

Apparently.

Goldie reappears in the window and hisses, "He's here!"

"Who?" I know who. But for some reason, I need to pretend I don't.

"*Him!* Officer Reid!"

My heart thumps far too much inside my chest. Perfect. The painfully hot man himself, come to haunt me in my place of business. Fantastic.

Goldie harbors no such qualms like mine, and why should she? Like her name, she is the golden girl no one can resist, and her blue eyes are bright with excitement. She fluffs her ponytail and wiggles her fingers. "Wish me luck!"

I twist my lips. "You need no such thing."

She giggles and does a miniature bow, then speeds away to flirt while I focus on the line of tickets in front of me.

"Burgers up," Dad says.

I turn and grab the plates, garnish them, and hit the bell. "Order up!"

One of the other servers, Melanie, appears and takes the food. She's replaced in seconds by Goldie, who's smiling even wider now.

"Oh my gosh, he's so *cute*," she sighs. "Have you seen him, Willa? The greenest eyes. His tan…and those *dimples*! Oooh, I wonder if he has those mirrored sunglasses. Maybe he'll stop me for speeding and say, 'Do you know how fast you were going?' in this really deep voice before whipping them off and staring into my soul like a sexy beast."

I ding the bell in her face. Twice. "Give me his order and get out of my window."

She blinks, then laughs, completely unfazed by my aggressive bell-dinging. "Okay, yeah, you've seen him. Here's the order."

I take the ticket she slaps down and start reading it off like always. "Dash Burger, hold the fried egg and avocado, add lettuce, tomato, onion." I stop, then read the ticket again. That's a regular burger.

Behind me, Dad replies, "So, a regular burger?"

"Guess so." I mutter, then yell through the window. "Hey, Goldie!"

My sister comes back. "What's up?"

I wave the ticket. "It's a regular burger. Just change the order."

She shakes her head. "Nope. I asked him the same thing. He wants the Dash Burger, hold the fried egg and avocado, add lettuce, tomato, onion."

Exhaling, I push the ticket into the holder. "Fine."

Except it's not fine, because it frazzles me so much I get the next order totally wrong, and Melanie's back in the window pointing at the table of middle-aged women and saying they want their orders completely re-done. Because of course they do.

You know what's worse than a table full of middle-aged women saying they want their orders completely re-done?

Nothing. There is absolutely nothing worse. Ask me how I know.

I've had it. Enough with this man and his stupid order and his stupidly pretty face.

Unwrapping my apron, I stalk out of the kitchen and find the source of the past seventy-two hours of frustration. Or maybe more. I've lost the ability to count thanks to this man. It's easy enough to spot him in the dining area: He's the guy in the navy-blue uniform that fits him like a freaking glove. The guy who is completely ignoring me as I approach and is chatting it up with his table mate, Ox Hall, another officer.

I point at him with a shaky finger, only this time the shakiness is from how mad I am. "You."

He startles and looks up, a question in his eyes. Then his entire expression morphs, and he smiles knowingly. "Hi."

I don't bother with pleasantries. "Just order the regular burger, *Officer*."

"But I—"

"Nope. No buts. It's the regular burger. Why do you need to order the Dash Burger if all you want is the regular one?"

Ox stifles a laugh, and he doesn't try holding back the grin when I glare at him. "Afternoon, Willa."

Not bothering to respond, I swivel my head back to Reid. "Well?"

Reid says, "What does it matter? You're not waiting on me, right?"

I cross my arms and try hard not to yell. "I'm the cook, so yes. It matters."

"Wait, really?"

My eyes narrow into slits. "What does that mean?"

"Sorry." He holds his hands up. "I didn't realize you were actually one of the cooks."

"Oh, man." Ox loses the battle and chortles.

"*Actually?*" I huff. "What does *that* mean?"

He shoots a helpless look at Ox, who's shaking with silent laughter. "I...I don't know. Sorry," he repeats, looking properly chastened.

It makes him hotter. And that makes me even angrier. "Listen, the Dash Burger is a specific burger. With a fried egg and guacamole. Do you have something against fried eggs?"

"No."

"Guacamole?"

"No, I—"

"But you want a burger with tomato, lettuce, and onion," I state. Honestly, I'd like to shut myself up at this point, but we're way too far gone.

"Right."

I wave the ticket at him. "Then why. Are. You. Ordering. The. Dash. Burger?"

Ox is practically melting into his side of the booth at this point.

Meanwhile, Officer Dimples lets out a defeated sigh. "I don't like sesame seeds," he mutters.

"You don't like—wait." I take a beat. "What?"

He straightens and clears his throat. "Sesame seeds. I hate the way they get caught in my teeth. The regular burger has a sesame seed bun and—"

"The Dash Burger doesn't," I finish for him. Aren't I a peach? My cheeks blaze with mortification. Of course. Of *course*. I jerk my chin in a nod, and leave the table without another word.

And then I make the best damn burger possible. He's going to be amazed at how delicious it is. He'll never be able to eat another burger without comparing it to this one. For the rest of his life, I want this man thinking of *my* burger. It'll serve him right.

Dad eyes me the whole time, because I may or may not be a little aggressive with my movements, but he remains quiet. When I've plated and dressed the burger, I decide I'll be the one to take it out to him, along with Ox's chicken salad and fruit plate.

To his credit, the man doesn't so much as flinch when I show up. Instead, he smiles up at me, showing off those damn dimples. "Hi, Willa."

"No sesame seed bun." I slide the burger and fries onto the table.

I didn't think it was possible, but the dimples get even deeper. "Thanks."

Apparently I'm a sadist, because when I return to the counter, I watch him. He takes a bite, and it's the sexiest thing I've ever seen.

Dammit.

"Willa." Mom sidles up to me and waves her phone in my face. "Have I shown you the reviews of that new place up in Nashville? Looks like they're angling for a James Beard award."

I grit my teeth. "Nope, you haven't."

She points to the screen. "Look. Their menu sounds perfect for you. Even has some of the same items from your semester at—"

"I need to get back to work, Mom." I turn away without another word.

CHAPTER 4

REID

ANOTHER DAY, ANOTHER morning of pretending not to notice Willa Dash as she hides behind Agatha's car.

It's cute, really. *She's* cute. Completely adorable, in fact, how she contorts herself into the strangest possible positions to ensure that I don't see her. I do, of course. I see everything. I observe a great deal. I'd go so far as to call it a plethora. Like the generously curvy outline of her at night behind the blue and white checked curtains that are now constantly drawn in her kitchen. An outline that hints at a body I wouldn't mind getting to know better. And I hear far more than she probably realizes, too, including the way her voice cracks as she sings to the pop songs blaring through her house.

It's a gorgeous summer morning. The light blue sky is streaked with clouds that are burning away by the minute, and the salty air is thick with humidity. People smile and wave as I pass them on my short drive to the station. I give Uncle Jack crap about it, but Lucky, Alabama really is quaint as hell. The little downtown looks like everyone agreed on a coordinating beachy color scheme for the buildings, and the town square is meticulously manicured with flowers and plants that someone definitely spends time taking care of. There's a coffee shop, a bookstore, an ice cream shop, even a little sliver of a storefront proudly announcing weekend ghost tours that end, naturally, at the ice cream shop. There's a sense of community and pride and outright *kindness* around this place, and it's downright disconcerting.

I'm not used to nice. Nice is suspicious.

At the station, I poke my head into my uncle's office to say good morning.

He looks up. "Any news?"

We've already fallen into a pattern. "No word from Chief Muñoz," I answer. "You'll be the first to know."

He gives a jerk of his chin. "You're with Ox again."

I give him a salute and prepare for my shift. It took no time to get up and running with the station, and I'm not sure if it's because the town of Lucky just doesn't insist on a lot of paper-work and training for its temporary officers or if my uncle simply didn't bother. Either way, after a wave and chat with Betty Pierce at the station's front desk, Ox and I are heading out on foot. I like the guy, even though he let me crash and burn with Willa the other day. He's a big, burly fucker with dark red hair and a thick beard who absolutely lives up to his name. After a pit stop at the coffee shop, we continue down Arnold Avenue, one of several blocks' worth of tiny shops and boutiques. The town caters to the tourists who flood it over the summer, that much is certain.

"Officers, over here!" comes a lady's voice.

"Mrs. G, good to see you!" To me, Ox says, "Mrs. G owns the original Tourist Trap."

I grin as we near the woman, who straightens after writing on the sandwich board sign on the sidewalk. "Tourist Trap? That's the actual name of her shop?"

"Yes, it is," Mrs. G says proudly. "You must be Officer Reid. Your uncle's been bragging all over town about you."

We shake. "He neglected to mention all the lovely shop owners I'd meet."

The older woman blushes and swats at me. "You're a flirt. Good for you." She turns to Ox. "Come tell me what you think about these new T-shirts and stickers."

We go into the shop. It's a classic beachside tourist trap, living up to its name perfectly. Racks of beach-appropriate clothes are on one side, and shelves everywhere are stuffed with all manner of toys, hats, sunblock, shot glasses, thimbles, shells, and more, most of them themed for the beach generally or Lucky in particular. When Mrs. G leads us to the display she wants our opinion on, I laugh. *I got lucky in Lucky, Alabama,* they say. "Perfect."

Ox nods approvingly. "You'll definitely sell these."

We chat a bit longer, and it's more of the same: the weather, the tide, the tourists, the pier, and locals I don't yet know. This town is absolutely nothing like Miami. Not only is it filled with people who aren't plastic surgeried to within an inch of their lives, but the pace is so much slower. When I was a beat cop before going undercover, I was constantly moving from one issue to the next. But here, we've barely gotten any real calls.

In a way, it's refreshing. But it also makes my skin itch. I've got to be missing something. No town is this nice.

We say our goodbyes to Mrs. G and head back onto the street. And who should I spy with my little eye but Willa Dash herself, along with the waitress who waited on me the other day. Willa's in loose-fitting green shorts and a baggy shirt, and it does exactly nothing to detract from her appearance. Especially when she smiles at her sister. Holy shit. It's the first time I've seen her smile, and it's so carefree and happy. She's *beautiful.* I take a deep breath, reaching up to rub away the sudden tightness in my chest.

Ox leans in and lowers his voice. "The Dash sisters. You've met Willa, obviously. Goldie is who waited on us during the sesame bun incident."

"I'm never forgiving you for that."

He snorts. "You did it to yourself, man."

He has a point, but I'll never tell him.

"Anyway, Goldie's the younger one by a couple of years. They're close. Town always figured Willa would head off and make something of herself and Goldie would stay here. And Willa left for a minute. She was on this reality cooking show. She hates talking about it."

My interest is piqued. "You're nothing more than a town gossip," I rib him.

He purses his lips. "Gotta do something to stay occupied. I regret nothing."

Willa and Goldie spot us simultaneously, the smile dropping from Willa's face as she freezes in place. Goldie grabs her hand to drag them across the street, making Willa stumble and flail to catch her footing. Goldie beams, throwing us a broad smile as they near.

"Officers Reid and Ox! What a pleasure."

"Good to see you, Goldie. Willa."

Goldie beams. Willa looks as though she'd prefer to crawl under a rock. "Afternoon, ladies." I tip my lukewarm coffee at them.

"You should really get a travel mug," Goldie says. "Come by the diner, and I'll gift you one of ours. It would be my pleasure."

I don't miss the barely disguised interest that Goldie's throwing my way, and as pretty and outgoing as she is, she might as well be invisible next to her sister. "Thanks. Maybe I'll do that. How are you, Willa?"

She blinks at me, surprised. "What?"

I smile, deliberately popping my dimples because I've seen how it flusters her. "I said, how are you?"

"Oh." She pushes her bangs out of her eyes and meets my gaze for a millisecond. With her dark hair and pale skin, her sky-blue eyes are startling. They're made even brighter by the blush that blooms on her cheeks as she fidgets. "Fine. Yep. I'm fine."

Goldie threads her arm through Willa's, giving her a

concerned look before turning her attention back to me. "You know, tomorrow's the First Friday Art Walk, Officer Reid. Do you like art?"

I tear my gaze away from Willa, who seems resolute in her mission not to meet my eyes. "Sure. I like art." I know nothing about art.

"You should come," Goldie purrs.

Ox coughs. Willa's cheeks blaze. And then I'm hit with what might honestly be the best idea of my life. YOLO and all that. "How about I take you ladies to the Art Walk?"

"Oh, that sounds wonderful!" Goldie enthuses, showing perfect white teeth.

"No," Willa practically shouts. "We...can't. That's...No."

Beside me, Ox swivels his head between all of us like it's some kind of three-way tennis match, and I know beyond a shadow of a doubt that he's enjoying this immensely.

I double down. "Why not? I should get to know the town more, and we're neighbors. It's a good plan."

"It's a *great* plan," Goldie corrects. "Seven o'clock?" When I nod, she says, "Perfect. We're looking forward to it, aren't we, Willa?"

Willa's not having it, and I almost want to take it all back at how uncomfortable she looks. "Not really," she mutters.

Goldie drags her away, mumbling something about sister wives.

Ox practically vibrates with laughter, and when they're finally out of earshot, he lets loose. "Oh, man, that was amazing," he says, wiping a tear from his eyes. "I can't wait to see this tomorrow. But Reid?"

"Yeah?"

"You have no idea what you're playing with. Goldie's a force."

Goldie isn't who I'm interested in. Not by a long shot. Besides, this is a short-term thing. What's the harm in a little fun?

CHAPTER 5

WILLA

I'M GOING TO kill my sister.

And my mother.

And Tom and Jerry.

Even Agatha, who I thought might actually be on my side with this whole ridiculous mess.

And I am *especially* going to kill my traitorous best friend, Matty. Who just FaceTimed me on his way back from visiting Farmer John about thirty miles north of here to inoculate all the cows.

Yes, Farmer John really is the man's name, bless his heart.

I'm about to lay into Matty for FaceTiming while he drives, because he knows good and well how I feel about that, but you know what? No. Maybe this way he'll have a tiny wreck. Bust a tire. *Then* there's a chance he won't be as into this stupid double-single date thing that Goldie's roped me into. Because when the hell has Goldie ever needed my help roping a man?

Never, folks. The answer is never. I am the opposite of helpful.

"Come on, Willa," Matty wheedles, giving me a view of his nostrils as he holds the phone and drives. "Just do it. What's the harm?"

"You have a booger in your nose."

He smirks and moves the mobile closer to his nose. "Wanna pick it?"

"You're disgusting."

He readjusts his hold and glances at me. "Come on, Willa. Be a good sport."

"Because being a good sport means looking like an idiotic third wheel on what is clearly a date for my sister?"

Matty makes a noise in the back of his throat.

"What was that?" I demand.

"What was what?"

"That noise. Did you just snort your snot?" I gag. "You're disgusting."

"It was just a noise!"

I point at the screen. "No. You've been a large animal vet for too long. You've gone to the dark side. You're snorting snot."

"Willa!" he laughs. "I wasn't…God, I can't even say it. *You're* disgusting."

"Fine. Then you made that noise on purpose. Why?"

Matty shrugs and grins. "Nothing, Willa. I was clearing my throat."

"Bullshit."

Goldie chooses that moment to FaceTime me as well. Rolling my eyes, I say, "Goldie's calling. Behave."

"Don't I always?" he asks with a mischievous smile.

"You do the opposite, Matthew John Brodigan." With that, I disconnect with him and accept the call with my little sister.

Her smile fills the screen, but I can still tell she's in her bedroom at our parents' house. Even though I couldn't wait to move out and get my own place, Goldie has no such desire. "What are you wearing?" she asks.

I angle the phone down so she can see. "Same as earlier."

She makes a face. "Absolutely not. Don't you have a dress?"

"Have you met me?" I don't care about clothes, and she

knows it. Most of mine smell like the diner, anyway, no matter how much detergent I put in the wash, so why bother? I mean, sure, I could wear chef's pants and tops in the diner, but one, it's a *diner*, and two, I haven't worn a chef's coat and pants since that disaster of a semester at the Culinary Institute of America.

Spend ten weeks getting followed around by a film crew you didn't know was going to be there, layer on top a chef whose anger and ego make Gordon Ramsay look like a kitten, and you get my illustrious CIA career. One that I have no intention of reviving. I'll be just fine here at the diner, thank you very much.

On the screen, the eye roll that Goldie gives me is Oscar-worthy. "Come on, Willa. Put in some effort. You wore that all day today."

"And why not keep wearing them?" My most comfortable shorts and a white T-shirt.

"Because you…never mind. Here's what I'm wearing." She pans the bed, and I see a summer yellow sundress. It'll be perfect on Goldie, with her tan skin and thick blond hair.

"Cute."

She turns the phone back on her face. "Exactly. And you need to look cute, too."

"This is your date, Goldie. Not mine."

"Then please, please, *please* wear something different. Show me what you've got."

Sighing, I heave myself up from my extremely comfortable couch and pad into my bedroom. I prop the phone on the dresser and open up a drawer.

"Pull out whatever's in there," Goldie prods. "No blind rummaging. I know you."

Damn. She really does. I pull all the contents of the drawer out and hold each item up for her inspection. Finally, a grueling fifteen minutes later, I have an outfit that meets with my sister's approval: cut-off jean shorts that I've had since high school and an emerald-green, unstained T-shirt that she's deemed acceptable.

She brings her phone close to her face and glares. "You better wear those."

I give the screen a mock salute. "Yes, ma'am."

Her left eye twitches, but she disconnects without another word.

I get dressed and shove my feet into my trusty Birkenstocks, then appraise myself in the mirror. I look fine. Hair is up in its customary ponytail, and hell, I'll even put some lip gloss on for Goldie. Done.

Then it's time to meet Reid outside. I take some centering breaths. This is all for my sister. I can definitely do this. The man is so handsome it nearly hurts to look at him, but for Goldie, I'll do it.

She owes me.

Big time.

Taking one last breath, I step out of my cottage and head around Agatha's to wait in her front yard. I don't know what to do with myself. We didn't talk about *where* to meet. Sure, technically the man lives next door, but am I supposed to go to his house and knock? I live *behind* Agatha's house. Was Reid supposed to leave his back door, cross the lawn and come to my place?

Crap. Maybe that's what was supposed to happen. But this isn't a date. Not for me, anyway. Not even close.

No, I was right to be out here.

I think.

I hate this.

I swivel on my heel, seconds from fleeing to the safety of my cottage, when I hear Reid's voice.

"Willa."

I jerk my head in his direction.

Oh, God.

I…I should never have agreed to this. Really glad I didn't shave my legs, because the sight of Reid is giving me goose-bumps, never mind that it's ninety-five degrees in the shade and, dear lord in heaven, today may be the day I'm leaving this mortal realm.

Because Reid is…well. He looks every bit the fancy man from Miami with his dark hair held back by a pair of sunglasses, a white collared button down fluttering over a fitted sky-blue tank that is definitely painted on, and white shorts that are just a smidge shorter than what I'm used to seeing on a man.

God *damn*. He is scrumptious. He's tomato pie and sweet iced tea on the porch with the ocean breeze ruffling your hair. He's Big Mama's banana pudding. He's the juiciest steak served perfectly off the grill.

Give me strength.

He smiles.

And my legs go weak. Again.

Then he looks up at me, his dimples popping. "Hi."

My knees weaken further, and as I begin to lose my fight with gravity, all I can think is, *well, at least he smiled at me*. Darkness begins to overtake me as Reid breaks into a run, his arms tightening around me to pull me upright just before I fall.

I force my eyes open as my heart rate kicks into high gear. My whole body shakes, and I'm not sure I can stand. "Mortified beyond recovery" doesn't really begin to describe what I'm feeling. I know one thing and one thing only: I would like to die now.

I am not just blushing the color of a tomato. I have turned into one. An overripe, gooey, just-this-side-of-becoming-sauce tomato.

"Are you okay?" The concern seeping through his voice isn't helping matters whatsoever. But then his face comes into focus, and his eyes are so pretty and green that I think maybe, perhaps, I can endure the burden of his presence just a little longer.

After I procure some kind of concoction that ensures he never, ever, ever, so help me *ever*, remembers this moment.

Like, ever.

"Willa?" he prompts again softly. You know what's not soft? His arms. The ones I'm currently wrapped inside. His muscles might have muscles.

"I'm...fine," I rasp. I'm definitely wrinkling his shirt.

Reid leads me to Agatha's porch steps and helps me sit on one of the wooden stairs, then takes my wrist in his hand to check my pulse.

I use the opportunity to study him. His hair, thick and wavy, is mussed to perfection, waving back from his brow as though an artist had spent hours styling it. His dark lashes are a thing of beauty. And have we talked about how freaking good he smells? Like honey in the forest. The combination shouldn't work, but it does. My lord, does it ever.

He looks at me with concern. "Your heartbeat is racing."

Yeah, no shit. It's because you're hot as hell, and I can't handle it.

"When was the last time you ate?"

I consider. Oh. My voice is small as I mutter, "This morning." That explains a lot.

I'm an idiot.

His face darkens. "We need to get some food in you."

Then he stands up. Before I can do the same, the man scoops me into his arms. Just, *boop!* Scoops me up, like I'm nothing.

Aaand holy cow, his muscles are legitimately bulging. My arms tighten around his on instinct, and I promise the warmth in my belly has nothing to do with my proximity to him.

Right?

Right.

He walks me back to his place, unlocking the door and walking us into the kitchen, still carrying me, as though I weigh no more than a sack of potatoes.

Which, honestly, is probably how sexy I am right now. Again:

I should have at least shaved. I did not. I refuse to look and see just how bad it is, but I'm absolutely positive he's getting some good exfoliation on the part of his arms that are touching my legs.

He deposits me onto a chair before I have a chance to get a good look at my surroundings.

"Coke?" comes his gruff voice.

I turn. He's got the refrigerator door open and is looking back at me, worry still plastered all over him.

"Do you have any tea?"

An amused smile drifts across his lips. "Willa. Do I look like the kind of guy who has iced tea in his fridge?"

No, you look like the kind of guy who might tie me up and spank me for misbehaving. I shake my head to get rid of the thought. "Coke is fine."

He pulls a can out and pops the tab with a hiss and a pop, then sets it on the tiny table in front of me. "You like Little Debbie?"

I scoff. "I am a southern woman, Reid. Of course I like Little Debbie."

He smiles again, much broader this time, but thank God not enough to make one of those illegal dimples appear. "Oatmeal Cream Pie?"

I nod and answer, "Roll Tide," referencing the Alabama football coach who was known to eat at least one of them a day.

He blanches. "I'm going to pretend you didn't just say that."

I narrow my eyes at him. "Think carefully before you answer this question: Where did you go to school?"

He smirks. *Smirks!* "Florida."

I swear on a stack of Little Debbies, I almost throw up in my mouth. "As in...the Gators?" I choke out.

He folds his arms over his chest, the move serving only to bring my attention to his incredibly defined forearms. Which, I'd just like to say, I didn't even know could be a thing. Since when do forearms distract me? "Yes, as in the Gators."

I grimace, but inwardly I'm practically doing jumping jacks. *Finally*, I've found a flaw in this man. "I'm not sure we can be friends, Reid."

He holds up the snack. "But I have Little Debbie."

I grin, unable to help myself. "Give it here and I'll reconsider."

Something like surprise flits across his face before he tosses it to me and I catch it, despite my shakiness. I unwrap it and take a bite, glad for the sugar that immediately hits my bloodstream. "Thanks," I mutter around a mouthful of sugary deliciousness.

"Anytime," he answers.

He's quiet while I snarf the snack, but to be fair, it's not like that takes a long time. I chug a few sips of the Coke and start to feel better.

"Color's coming back," he observes, pulling out the chair across from me and studying me the way a doctor would a patient.

"Sorry about that." I swallow the last of the delicious goodie and pull out my phone. "I should text Goldie."

He nods, and I send a message telling her what's happened.

GOLDIE

Are you okay?

I'm fine.

I don't tell her how embarrassed I am.

GOLDIE

Still coming?

I look up at Reid, then back to my phone.

Still coming.

Reid keeps his hand at the small of my back as we walk to his car, and I have to force myself not to swoon at the move. First, he scoops me into his arms and carries me inside his house, and now he's guiding me to his truck. Which doesn't really match with the rest of him, if I'm being honest.

He gets into the cab's driver seat and starts the truck up.

"Is this new?" I ask.

"The truck?"

I nod. "It doesn't have that new car smell, but you don't look like a Ford 250 kind of guy, I've gotta be honest."

He chuckles and steers us onto the street. "And what kind of guy do I look like?"

I consider. "A Mustang," I finally say. "A black one. With a really loud muffler or whatever, so that everyone hears you coming. And a vanity plate."

He straight up guffaws, the laugh emanating from deep within his belly, and I'd be lying if I said it didn't make me feel some kind of way to hear it. And to know that I did it.

I shake myself free of the thoughts. This is a date for my sister. I'm just the third wheel. We meet up with Goldie after Reid parks the truck, and we walk to the coffee shop.

"Need more to eat?" Reid asks, his attention never really straying from me. Which is weird because Goldie looks pretty as a picture in her sunshine-yellow dress and curled hair hanging down her back.

Goldie looks at me sharply. "Are you okay?"

I shrug, a little embarrassed at the fuss they're making over me. "I'm fine. No need to worry about me—let's go to Marnie's Art Shop first."

But Goldie's not having it. "You definitely need to eat. I can see it all over your face. What did you give her?" Her tone is sharp.

Reid doesn't miss a beat. "Oatmeal Cream Pie and a Coke."

Her eyes bug out. "Seriously?"

He shrugs. "She nearly fainted, and it's what I had to offer."

Goldie threads her arm through mine. "Come on. You need actual food, and then we'll do the art walk."

I let myself be led away, and after a quick meal of sandwiches and tea at the coffee shop, we head out to the main section of downtown where the art is. It's one of my favorite weekends of the month, and I don't get to go nearly as much as I'd like to. Working as Dad's only other main cook has its advantages, but there are plenty of disadvantages, too. Namely, not being able to take off every weekend like I would if I had a more regular job. Then again, what's the fun in a regular job? Besides, it's not like I'd know what a "regular job" was if it walked up and introduced itself to me.

Goldie positions Reid between the two of us, which makes no sense. Unfortunately, Reid's giant form blocks me from looking at my sister and eyeing her. I peel off to a pop-up booth on the sidewalk at my earliest opportunity, and in between inspecting the handmade wooden spoons that should really be on display in a gallery and not be for sale to use willy-nilly like this, I hiss at Goldie. "What are you doing?"

She looks at me, the picture of innocence. "What are you talking about?"

I set a spoon down and cross my arms. "Putting Reid between us. We're here for you, not me."

Her eyes widen. "Willa, we're just showing our new police officer around town. He needs friends."

I make a noise of disgust and turn around, knocking right into the man of the hour's very formidable—and very solid—chest.

"Oof," I breathe out, unable to help myself from flattening my hands on that awesome chest we just reviewed.

Holy muscles. Again. I should be used to this by now, but alas, I am not.

"You okay?" he asks, his hands steadying me as I rock back on my heels.

No. No, I am not okay. Because once again, I am assaulted by him and his muscles and his ridiculous cedar-y masculine scent, and it's unholy the way my body is reacting, thanks. Never in my life have I had an overwhelming need to confess my sins to someone, but right now? Have mercy.

Again.

Basically, I need everything to stop because I cannot with this. I'm not even mad about it anymore. Just begging for it to stop.

"Willa?"

I blink. "I'm fine. Can we go?"

"Of course." He gestures for me to go ahead of him, and I swear I feel the heat of his hand over my lower back as I weave through the crowd to return to the street.

Goldie joins us, once more positioning Reid between me and her, and we continue our stroll down the street. I feel utterly foolish, and I'm positive the heat on my cheeks is not, in fact, from the sun.

A click sounds a few feet away, and I startle. There, inspecting the screen on his massive camera, is none other than JJ Jennings, looking pleased as punch at the photo he's snapped.

"Nolan Jennings, Junior, *Lucky Herald*," he says, sticking out a hand as he moves toward us. "Everyone calls me JJ."

Reid takes it, mercifully stepping forward a bit and giving me the distance I need to be able to freaking breathe.

As I gulp in deep breaths of non-Reid scented air—glorious, glorious plain ocean air—JJ is performing his standard spiel for all who have the misfortune of becoming the focus of his interest.

"Owner and proprietor of the paper, of course. You know how hard it is these days to be a small paper. Tough. Gotta do what needs to be done to keep providing the news to the people, you understand."

Reid's eyes have glazed over in the few seconds JJ's been at it, and even Goldie seems a little dazed. I take a last heaving gulp of fresh air and step forward, hoping that Reid's scent will have somehow dissipated in the short time we've not shared the same square footage.

"Okay, JJ." I step between the men and take small sips of air. "He gets it. You've not even let him introduce himself."

JJ waves me off. "I know who he is. What I really want to know is how he managed to get out here with both Dash women."

Reid flashes him a teasing grin, one of his dimples showing. "Lucky, I guess." Then he turns to me and Goldie. "Ladies, shall we?"

Goldie brandishes her own smile. "Absolutely. But we should give JJ what he wants."

We each take an arm and pose. Reid is gorgeous, Goldie is her usual confident self, and I probably look like a troll. Can't wait to see this story in the next edition.

Chapter 6

Reid

I FINISH TYING my laces and step outside the house, pretending as usual that I don't see Willa as she squeaks and runs behind Agatha's car in the driveway. This woman has no chance of being stealthy. She *has* to know I know she's there, so why she insists on acting like she's invisible is a complete mystery. But it's cute. *She's* cute.

She peeks around the car's bumper, and while it takes everything in me not to wave at her, I continue my warmup to give her the illusion of control. She remains where she is as I jog down the stairs and kick into a run, heading deeper into the small neighborhood. Behind me, I hear the unmistakable click of a car door opening, and I grin as I spin to watch her scramble inside and start the engine.

Willa speeds off in the other direction, and I resume my run. This whole first week has been a whirlwind of getting used to the place. It turns out there's a little more action in a small town than I figured there would be, but the action isn't exactly what I expected. I have climbed a fire truck ladder to "rescue" a cat from its perch way up in a tree in the town square because the usual guys weren't able to do it. (They were perfectly capable, of course; they liked watching me try to get a cat to do something it didn't want to.) I've cited no less than twenty people for not having the requisite license to fish off the pier. I've checked the historical schoolhouse for a security breach, and I've reset the clock in the square—twice—from where it's perpetually three minutes ahead. I can't decide if it makes me miss Miami more or less.

I am absolutely certain this is Lucky's way of hazing me, and honestly, it's hard not to be charmed by it. The people themselves are far too nice, and even the tourists aren't that bad. I'm definitely used to a...*different* pace in Miami. One that is much, much faster. A big perk to this temp gig is that it's mainly day shifts. Sure, I've got to do some nights here and there, but considering I'm filling in for someone, it's surprising.

Turning the corner, I increase my pace, grateful for the flat roads and relatively smooth sidewalks. Hell, I'm grateful that I can run without worrying some lackey from the Bunnies is going to show up and try to harm me. Or worse.

To hear my uncle talk, this position could be permanent if I wanted. The woman I'm filling in for will be back, of course, but he says they could use another set of hands. It's tempting in a fantasy sort of way, because I can't imagine not living in Miami. What would I even do around here? There aren't a lot of restaurants, and there's only one movie theater, to start with.

The *real* perk so far, if I'm being honest, has been Willa. I chuckle and wipe the sweat from my brow. I did not see this woman coming. How could I? I've spent the past decade surrounded by plastic in all its glory—and listen, there's a lot to appreciate about how far plastic surgeons have taken their craft, no hate to the women and men who get work done—but Willa.

What a fresh breath of air.

Not gonna lie...I'm a little intrigued by her. Who wouldn't be? She's kind of a mess, but it's adorable. The way she squeaks and increases her speed to get into her house *every single afternoon* when I say hi to her from my backyard? The way she keeps hiding in the mornings and thinking I don't see her when she's leaving for work? The way she sings so badly in her house? There's something about her that has me wanting more.

The art walk on Friday was something else. Willa did everything in her power to stay away from me so I could have time with Goldie, but I wanted time with her. Time she seemed determined not to give. Everyone seemed to know everyone, and they had warm smiles for Willa and Goldie, and flat-out curious ones for me.

And JJ. That ridiculous excuse for a journalist immediately had us on the front page of the town's weekly newspaper. Although "newspaper" is a little aggressive for the rag. It's a gossip column with a few advertisements here and there from local shops. And it's six pages, tops. No wonder print journalism is having a tough time of it if people like JJ Jennings are the main source of it.

And if they have some kind of town Facebook page? Forget about it. I don't ever want to know.

I turn another corner, this time back in the direction of my rental. I've already decided where I'm eating lunch.

IT'S NOT HARD TO CONVINCE UNCLE JACK TO JOIN ME at the diner. At precisely twelve-forty-five, we're bellying up to the counter, and my uncle is in full-fledged Chief Mac mode. Tom and Jerry, who I'm willing to bet are the source of most of JJ's "articles," eye me around Chief's back. "How's your first week been?"

I think of Willa, the cat, the clock, and all the fishing citations. "Interesting," I decide to say.

Jerry chuckles. "I bet."

"Seems like the clock is running ahead again." Tom glances outside as if he can see it.

Spoiler alert: he can't. Not only does the man wear glasses as thick as old Coke bottles, it's also near the center of the town square, which isn't remotely visible from here.

I grin. "Is it, now?"

Barbara shuffles over to us from behind the counter, her warm smile just like Goldie's. "Good to see you, boys. Coffee?"

Chief says yes, but I ask for water. I look around Barbara and see Dean in the window. We exchange nods as he looks back down to his work.

A curse comes from the kitchen, and I know without question that it's Willa. I can't help the smile on my face, because I'm willing to bet she's cussing at my appearance. I have never had this effect on anyone, and I absolutely love it.

The thing is, she doesn't realize the effect she has on me.

When Barbara takes my order, I make certain to order the Patty Melt, then add guacamole and a fried egg just to rile Willa up.

Sure enough, Barbara sticks the order in the window and Willa is the one to grab it. Her hair is up in its customary ponytail, bangs hanging just a little too far into her pretty blue eyes, and her cheeks flush as she reads the ticket. The woman must be terrible at poker. She growls—it's impossible not to hear it—and when she unleashes her glare out of the window, I'm right there to catch it.

I smile and wave.

I didn't think it would be possible, but her cheeks get even brighter as her eyes widen. She's been caught, and she looks embarrassed.

Yeah, she's cute as hell.

My order comes exactly as I requested, and I'm almost disappointed she didn't stomp around to drop it in front of me. But I take a bite, and I swear, this woman's cooking skills are beyond this diner. She belongs in some kind of fancy restaurant, with little cook minions running around and muttering "Yes, Chef" to her every whim. It's obvious.

When I'm certain she's not paying attention to me, I say to Barbara, "I heard Willa studied at the Culinary Institute of America."

Barbara's face lights up. "Oh, yes! She did. Came back after just a few months, but we'd all love to see her go back. Get out of this town and really spread her wings, you know?"

"She's fine," Tom grumbles.

Barbara waves Tom off. "Ignore him. My daughter is too brilliant to be stifled by this town, aren't you, Willa?" She directs that last part through the open window right as the woman in question slides an order toward her.

Willa raises her eyebrows. "I like it here, Mom."

"You do not," Barbara responds.

"I do."

"No, you don't." Barbara frowns at Willa before turning back to me. "What are your plans while you're here, Reid?"

There's no mistaking the shift in her tone, and it's one I've learned to identify well over the years: the Interested Mother of a Single Daughter. I adjust my seat and swallow the bite of Patty Melt that has no right tasting as good as it does.

"Just here to do my job, ma'am."

She blushes and waves a rag at me. "Don't call me ma'am—makes me feel old." Then she leans in closer. "Didn't you have a good time with Goldie at the art walk?"

And there it is. Make no mistake about it: For as much as Willa—and apparently Barbara—wants it to happen, Goldie had no more interest in me than I did in her. It was obvious. But small town or not, I know enough about families to realize that if Goldie's not saying anything to her mom, neither will I. I offer up a noncommittal grunt, then kick my uncle's leg to get his attention.

Chief Mac isn't about to come to my rescue. He does the exact opposite. "Nothing wrong with a few dates while you're here, Reid," he says merrily. "And who knows? Maybe you'll end up staying."

I glare at him and make a mental note to take him off my Christmas list. "Right," I drawl, then shove another bite of food in my mouth.

"Oh, wouldn't that be exciting?" Barbara grabs the water pitcher to offer us all refills. "Having you here permanently will be wonderful."

I don't miss the way Willa's attention perks up. I also don't miss the way her shoulders droop infinitesimally when I say, "Just here for three months, ma'am."

Chapter 7

Willa

I'M PREPARED FOR my usual, incredibly humiliating yet completely unavoidable reaction to Reid when I get home: a horrified squeak that emanates from the depths of embarrassment hell, followed by a stumbling dash inside my cottage. But for once, he's not lounging in the Adirondack in his backyard, strumming a guitar like some hot fantasy come to life. I slow to a stop and stare at the empty chair, trying desperately to ignore the feeling that's in my chest. A feeling I'd rather not name, thank you very much.

Get over yourself, Willa. He's not interested in me, despite the way I've caught him looking. He's confused. *I* confuse him. That has to be what's happening. It's the only reason a man would willingly ignore the signs that Goldie is giving him. Maybe he thinks I'll turn into some weird stalker? For all the sense that makes.

But even Goldie's being weird. As though her flirting with him is just standard. A reflex that she does out of habit and nothing more. Now that I think about it, she stopped talking about how good-looking he was after the art walk.

Huh.

I push back into gear, walking into my little home and peeling off my clothes as I go, sighing in relief at being able to drop them in my usual trail.

After taking a shower and towel-drying my hair, I throw on some ratty yoga pants and a threadbare shirt that hangs off my shoulder, revealing the faded sports bra that's seen way better days, I shove my feet into Birkenstocks and head the ten yards or so to Agatha's back door. I eat over here about once a week, but for once, she told me I wasn't going to be the one cooking. Which is a little concerning—Agatha isn't the best cook—but it's impossible to resist being fed a meal I didn't have anything to do with.

I open the door and am immediately hit with the scent of something delicious. Butter, onions, garlic: the holy trinity of cooking, as far as I'm concerned.

"Agatha, this smells amaz—" I stop speaking as soon as I round the corner, the words stuck in my throat.

Standing in front of the stove, normal as you please, is Reid Dimples MacKinnon.

Cooking.

Of course.

Because why wouldn't I throw on the absolute worst outfit and then see the hottest man on the planet?

My cheeks flame, sending heat down my neck and even to the shoulder exposed to the air. I heave a resigned sigh. "Reid."

Tongs in hand, he turns, his eyes raking over me from head to toe. The goosebumps rising in the wake of his review are plenty enough proof of how my traitorous body feels about his perusal. It's probably not even a second of time, but it may as well be an eternity. I now have a deep, palpable understanding of how a rabbit in the wild must feel when it stills in the presence of a predator, muscles tense and eyes and ears alert, hopeful that if it stays still, the predator won't sense them. What the rabbit doesn't realize, perhaps, is that its fear only heightens the predator's pleasure in the hunt.

Reid flashes what I'm beginning to think of as his signature smile, making both dimples pop. A predator, indeed. "Evening, Willa Dean."

I swallow. "Just Willa."

"Evening, Just Willa," he shoots back, not hesitating.

Agatha approaches with a glass of white wine and shoves it into my hands. "Drink, dear. You look a little peaked."

I turn my glare on the old woman and lean in to whisper. "You could have warned me."

She titters delightedly, her pale blue eyes bright behind chunky, red-framed glasses. "And miss the fireworks? Not a chance."

I swear Reid chuckles under his breath, but the sizzling of the pork as it hits the pan to sear drowns the sound out.

So, let's recap: He's hot, he's got muscles and dimples for days, he wears a uniform to work, he lives next door, he plays the guitar, he's nice to old ladies, and he cooks for them, too.

Fantastic.

Great.

Love this for me.

I take another gulp of wine and gesture for Agatha to get a refill ready. I'm going to need it.

Agatha keeps a steady chatter going the entire time Reid works, and despite myself, I inch closer to watch. I can't help it. Call it professional curiosity.

It certainly has nothing to do with the way his muscles flex as he sautés the spinach. I'm merely interested in how he tests the temperature of the pork. That's the only reason I'm this close.

"I promise I won't serve undercooked pork, Chef," Reid says, winking at me.

The heat in my cheeks is only from the wine. Period.

Also, the butterflies that just took flight in my stomach at him calling me *Chef?* Coincidence.

I cough, unable to even believe myself. I take a healthy step back, not really understanding how I let myself get this close. Forget predator. The man is a freaking vampire. Don't they, like, lure you to them or something? "I—I trust you," I stammer.

He raises a perfect eyebrow. "Do you? Trust me?" His voice dips low as he speaks, and damn if I don't bend a little closer to hear him.

Crap! I'm doing it again. Swallowing, I straighten and take yet another very firm, very deliberate step away. "Of course. Seems like you know your way around the kitchen."

He presses a knuckle to the pork, nods, then pulls the towel off his shoulder and opens the oven to stick the entire pan in.

Listen, I know I said watching him eat my food was the sexiest thing I'd ever seen.

I was wrong.

Watching him *cook* is the sexiest thing I've ever seen.

"You're staring," he whispers teasingly, shutting the oven door and flipping the towel back over his shoulder in what's clearly a practiced move.

Mother. Fucker.

My face is flaming, and I should probably admit to myself that it's not the wine.

I will do no such thing.

Instead, I shrug. "It's just nice for someone else to cook for me, that's all."

"Is that all?"

I nod decisively and repeat it. "That's all."

He studies me, and as his mossy-green eyes flit from one part of my face to the other, I have no doubt he knows I'm lying.

Agatha, the conniving minx, stays uncharacteristically silent while Reid and I have...whatever it is we're having.

When dinner is ready, Reid plates the meals as carefully as if he's cooking in a five-star restaurant, using the towel to wipe off excess sauce. He serves Agatha first, then me, before bringing his own plate to the table.

This asshole.

My throat thickens at the beauty of the presentation. Beautifully cooked medallions of pork tenderloin lie on a bed of sautéed spinach and risotto, with thinly-sliced ribbons of carrots coiled perfectly to the side. A dollop of cranberry compote is to the side as well. The display is top tier. I have never put this much effort into a meal for Agatha, and twin feelings of shame and competition roar to the surface.

"Oh, Reid, what a treat!" Agatha says as she takes in the food. "Don't you think this is wonderful, Willa?"

Both of them look at me expectantly as I unfold my napkin and lay it on my lap. "Beautiful," I agree, my voice remarkably even.

We dig in, and I take it all back. Because *now* he's the asshole. The pork is fucking perfect, evenly seared on the outside, tender and juicy on the inside. I couldn't improve on it if I wanted to, and that pisses me off.

What can I say? I'm a perfectionist.

Thankfully, the risotto is fine. Well, it's more than fine, but I can make a better risotto. The spinach is perfect, not too overdone and not too garlicky.

"What do you think, Chef?" Reid asks.

Those stupid butterflies take off again at the moniker. "It's… really good," I grudgingly admit.

The smile on his face is enough to melt my panties. There's pride and accomplishment, and he's freaking *beaming*. "Really?"

"Are you kidding? You know you're a good cook," I say, then I shovel another bite into my mouth. Ugh. Delicious. All of it. I hate it.

He's still smiling. "That's high praise, coming from you."

I blink. Does he—does he actually care what I think? Impossible.

We finish dinner, Agatha keeping a steady stream of chatter going about the various goings-on around town.

Reid excuses himself to go to the restroom, and I whirl on Agatha. "You have a lot of nerve, you know that?"

She is wholly unrepentant. "Willa Dean Dash, you need out of this town. Who better to whisk you away than that young man? Start something up with him and when his time is up, you'll go to Miami with him. Get a job at a real restaurant." She takes her plate and walks the few steps into the kitchen, the subject as good as closed.

I growl. "Agatha, I've *told* you that I like it here!"

She sets the dish in the sink and holds her hand out for mine. "How can you know you like it here when the only time you left was one semester of cooking school? You've not been anywhere, Willa."

I barely hold back a scream. *One semester of cooking school?* She makes it sound like I was in regular college, doing regular college stuff, when the experience was far more brutal and cutthroat than that. I'm about to retort, but Reid's steps tell me he's nearly back to the kitchen. And I'm not having this conversation for the millionth time with Agatha. She and everyone else are convinced that all I need is to get out of town. What no one bothers to consider is my feelings on the matter.

Reid insists on helping with clean-up, and we have the kitchen set to rights quickly. I'm about to suggest we open another bottle of wine when Agatha claps her hands, an expectant look on her face. "Well, I'm exhausted. Time for bed. I'll see you kids later!"

I narrow my eyes. "Agatha, you always insist on me staying to watch *Jeopardy!* And that doesn't come on for another —"

"As I said, I am exhausted." She grabs my arm and turns me toward the back door, and holy wow, she is *strong*.

"Do you lift weights?" I ask.

She rolls her eyes. "Child, I swear. You exhaust me. Get out of here." Then she turns to Reid. "Walk her home."

Reid is clearly aiming for favorite neighbor status, because he simply nods. "Of course. Thanks for having me over."

"Thanks for cooking," she responds, opening the door and practically shoving us onto the white slats of the front porch before shutting the door with more force than is necessary.

Reid turns his knowing gaze to me, bemused. "She's fun."

I chuckle, grateful to realize that I'm not terrified of him right now. And hey, it only took two glasses of wine.

I should probably think a little critically about why I need a drink or two to be comfortable around Hottie McGee here, but I'm just going to move past it. "She is," I agree. "And you don't have to walk me home—it's literally thirty seconds away."

He shakes his head seriously. "Absolutely not. I promised. And I'm an officer of the law."

"How does that play into this, exactly?"

He grins, his lips far too luscious for any sane person to bear. "It's in the oath we take."

"You solemnly swear to keep all promises made to old ladies?"

His smile is bright enough to rival the sun. "Precisely."

Managing not to swoon, and being unreasonably proud of that fact, I shrug and start toward my door as Reid talks and smiles. While walking me home...all fifty or whatever feet of it. The cicadas are out in force, and a breeze brings the salty scent of the ocean with it. I slow my pace, wanting to extend the moment just a little longer.

Actually, what I really want to do is sit and turn this night over, sifting through the moments, reflecting on the company and the food.

Reid, ever the observant one, notices. "You want to sit?" He gestures at the chairs in his backyard.

I shake my head. "No, it's just..." I trail off and barely repress a sigh.

"Just what?" he prods gently.

Be brave, Willa.

I take a breath and hope my voice is steady when I speak. "I really like sitting outside on my porch there." I point to the joke of a porch that juts off the kitchen and faces his property.

"Now?"

I hum. "Other times, too. But you're always in the yard, and you're...*you*...and I really only need like thirty minutes."

He grins, and so help me, if he presses me on what I mean by *you're you*, I might go up in flames. He licks his lips, and something tightens inside me. "So, what, you want me to go inside my house for half an hour while you have some time to yourself on your porch?"

I nod, feeling my cheeks heat again. "Just from four to four-thirty."

His lips quirk up. "That specific, huh?"

I sound ridiculous. I pull my shirt up for the millionth time that night, attempting and immediately failing to cover my shoulder. Reid's eyes flit to the exposed skin as I say, "You know what? Never mind. It's silly, and I can deal—"

"I'll do it," he says gruffly, dragging his gaze back.

I stare up at him. "You—you'll do it?"

He does that thing again where he seems to take in each part of my face, from my eyebrows to my chin and every millimeter of skin in between. It's unnerving. "You deserve whatever you want, Willa." His voice is rough.

I lick my lips, and he follows the movement.

A flash of lightning streaks across the sky out of nowhere, and with it comes the realization that this man might actually see me as more than Willa Dean Dash, sheltered daughter of Barbara and Dean Dash and sister of Goldie. He doesn't see the awkward girl from the reality cooking show who got yelled at so badly that she came running home to hide in her parents' diner. He sees...me.

So, I do the dumbest thing I've ever done in my life. Instead of turning to run, which is definitely what should be happening, I give voice to the one thing I want. "Kiss me."

He tilts his head, studying me. "Kiss you?"

I stand taller. "Yeah. Kiss me."

"Why?"

"Why not? Isn't it what Agatha wants?" *What I want?*

He smirks, the peacock in him evident. "First, you shouldn't base your actions on what others want. Second, I don't think you're ready for this."

My cheeks heat once more, this time with the sting of his rejection. I was wrong. So wrong.

He doesn't want me. If anything, he probably feels sorry for me, and he certainly doesn't want to make Agatha mad. Who would? I nod. "Okay, got it. I'll just—" I start to go around him, but he grabs my arm and spins me to him.

I slam into his chest, the masculine scent of him immediately surrounding me. His eyes are molten. "Willa," he says. "I told you that you deserved whatever you wanted."

Then his lips meet mine.

Heaven opens, angels sing, the whole thing. There might be another strike of lightning, or it might be my brain exploding.

I can affirmatively state that movies and books haven't gotten kisses right. They're not even on the same planet as what's happening with this kiss.

Because this is something from an entirely different galaxy.

His hands wrap around me, one on my waist and one cupping my chin, both of them pressing in. Instead of feeling trapped, I feel as though I'm being held for the first time. His scent, cedar and honey tasted at the height of summer, surrounds me like always. I hear the cicadas again. I'll never be able to separate the sound from this feeling.

In mere seconds, Reid has completely ruined me for anyone else. There's a sense of safety within his arms, against his chest. Like this man would do anything for me. It's intoxicating. His hand slides down to my rear and squeezes, and I slide mine beneath his shirt. His skin is smooth, the muscles compact and tense under my touch. Our chests heave, and I'm moments away from begging him to come inside my house and continue the kiss.

Then he slants his mouth over mine and pushes his tongue in, making me see stars. He tastes like the wine we had with dinner, and as his tongue slides across my own, his stubble scrapes deliciously around my lips. His thumb traces circles over my chin that feel erotic.

This isn't real.

It can't be real.

I break the kiss, both of us breathing hard. He tips his forehead to mine, his eyes searching for…I have no idea what.

But I do know that I need to be done. That I need to stop the dream before it's ripped out of my grasp. I pull my hand away from the glory that is his chest and step back. "Thanks."

"*Thanks?*" The disbelief in his voice is evident.

"Yeah. Thanks." And before either of us can say another word or make another move, I swivel and go inside.

I race to my bedroom, flopping onto the bed and burying my face in my pillow.

What have I done?

CHAPTER 8

WILLA

MATTY AND I have a Sunday ritual: yoga at the downtown studio, then iced coffee from the shop across the street, then we walk along the pier. We've done it for years, and it's pretty sacred at this point. The pelicans and seagulls swoop and dive around us, the pelicans hunting for actual fish and the seagulls looking for the chips and snacks the tourists are bound to drop. Off to one side of the pier, a line of beautiful sailboats and catamarans bounce and bob in the water, gleaming in the sunlight and waiting on their owners to take them out.

Then there's me, griping about last night as Matty's eyes get wider and wider. "So, to be clear: you asked him to kiss you, and then you told him...thanks?"

"Yep."

"Sweetheart, I love you so much." The patience in his voice is admirable. "But what in the world were you thinking?"

I take another sip of my iced coffee, letting the cool liquid slide down my throat before I speak. "You don't understand. He was an asshole all through dinner, cooking this incredible meal,

being all competent and thoughtful, and the way he's so observant, Matty—it's unnerving."

"Well, he's a cop, so —"

"And then he had the gall to look at me. Like, really look at
me. As if he *saw* me."

Matty snorts. "The nerve."

"Exactly! The nerve." But he doesn't get it. "You don't understand. You're the only one who doesn't give me hell on a daily
basis to leave town."

"Because you're never leaving Lucky," Matty says simply.

I swat at his arm. "See? You know! Now, pretend that you've
gotten the kiss of your life by someone who hasn't known you for
a decade. Who has no experience of you as anyone other than the
person they're kissing. And it blows your mind. And then they
look at you."

He quirks a smile and looks at me, his brown eyes twinkling,
but also soft with understanding. "And he really saw you,
didn't he?"

I gulp my coffee and nod. "And then yesterday? He was
nowhere to be found. Usually, I have to do this whole hide-and-
seek thing to not be seen by him, but yesterday? Nowhere. Was
the kiss so bad that he went back to Miami?"

Matty pulls me into a side hug, his lean frame nothing like the
solid wall of muscle I was wrapped in the other night, and
gestures to the open bench facing the ocean. "Let's sit."

"I'm embarrassed and turned on and confused and I don't ever
want to see him again, and also I really, really want to kiss him
again. A lot." There's no stopping the way I'm whining.

Matty nods. "I can help you out on yesterday, Willa. He was
working his tail off. Pretty sure the residents of Lucky are still
attempting to haze him."

Confused, I narrow my eyes at Matty. "Haze him?"

He chuckles and finishes his coffee with a slurp before turning to toss it into the garbage can nearby. "Yep. More time here at the pier —and don't freak out, he's not here right now—and I'm pretty sure he had to power wash a block of sidewalk over on Sequoia, and then of course he was answering the phones at the station overnight."

I consider all this. "Yeah, not helpful. I'm still feeling all the feelings." Besides, he was probably grateful for all the work. Then he wouldn't have to face me and what he probably thinks is a terrible kiss.

Matty straightens and shields his eyes. "Did you hear that?"

I listen. "Is something squeaking?" Following the direction of his attention, I catch sight of something black and fuzzy in the shadow of another bench. "Oh, no. Matty, don't you dare get involved—"

But he's up and moving, the animal lover and vet in him roaring to the surface.

By the time I make it to him, he's already crouched and softly clucking his tongue at the creature. In seconds, he's unfurling himself from the ground, a tiny black kitten yowling plaintively in his large palms.

"Oh, Matty," I breathe, immediately turning to goo at the sight of the poor thing. "Is it going to be okay?"

"Hard to tell, honestly," he answers. "Come on."

Our walk forgotten, we head to Matty's car, and I hold the kitten as he drives us to his office. The little thing is panting and mewling, blinking blue-green eyes up at me as if I've wronged it by having the audacity to try to help save it. Which, truly, could not be more of a cat thing if it tried.

Matty takes the kitten from me before we even get out of the car. "Might be a broken leg," he murmurs, holding the ball of fur in a way that ensures it's as comfortable as possible.

I follow along, opening the office with the keys Matty hands me, and flipping on the lights as we go into one of the exam rooms.

Matty puts the kitten on the cold metal table and asks me to watch it, then leaves. He returns a few minutes later with a bunch of supplies that make my head swim: a bag of fluid, a razor, some gauze and tape, and other stuff I don't recognize. After palpating the kitten's leg gingerly, and the kitten protesting loudly about the unwanted attention, Matty nods and purses his lips. "It's not fully broken, but it's not great. I'm going to give it some fluids, something for the pain, and wrap it up. You want to stay and watch?"

I bolt without thinking twice. I don't want to see the poor thing in pain, and it's yowling loud enough that I'm fully aware of its displeasure, anyway.

Nearly an hour later, Matty and the kitten emerge, the floof blinking sleepily and its little back leg in a cast. My heart melts.

"Oh, the poor baby."

Matty cradles it against his chest. "She's going to be just fine. What she needs is some love and affection and she'll be right as rain." Then he looks at me. "Ready to go?"

I hold the little floof while Matty drives me home, petting its soft fuzz as we go.

By the time we get to my house, the kitten is asleep. Matty looks at me. "Guess the little girl is yours."

I jerk my head up, my eyes wide. "What? No way."

But he's already out of the car, deliberately ignoring my protests as he rounds the vehicle and opens my door. "Look how perfect she is with you."

"It's a girl?"

Matty nods. "Probably about ten weeks old. Which is good. She can eat regular food and everything."

I climb out of the car. "Yeah, no way, Matty. I can't take care of a kitten. Take it with you. Add it to your menagerie." I follow him around Agatha's house, still holding the floof like the precious cargo it is, and continue protesting. "You know what my hours are like. It's not fair to leave a little kitten alone for that long."

Matty gives me a look. "Willa. It's a *kitten*."

"Exactly!"

He sighs and takes the ball of fur from me. "Kittens become cats. Cats don't need much. It's the perfect animal for you. She's perfect." His tone shifts a little, but I don't bother trying to figure out why.

"You can't make me. Besides, doesn't it need, I don't know, pain killers?" I sound like a petulant toddler, but I can't find it within myself to care.

"*She* does, but it's not hard to give them to her. Why don't you get Reid to help?"

I gape at him. "Why would I do that?"

"Help with what?"

I whirl around, and standing behind me is none other than Reid MacKinnon.

I squeak. *SQUEAK*. The kitten doesn't react.

Can I please, for just once in my life, be normal around him? For God's sake, he's had his tongue in my mouth.

Speaking of mouths, his quirks up knowingly. "Hi, Willa Dean."

"Just Willa," I mumble.

His smile broadens. "Hi, Just Willa."

Matty watches the entire exchange with far more interest than a man in his late twenties should. "I was suggesting that maybe you'd help Willa take care of her new kitten."

"I didn't say I was keeping her!" I stomp my foot in emphasis.

Reid nods at the fuzzy bundle of fur in Matty's arms. "Is this our culprit?"

Matty steps closer to Reid. I wonder what it's like to behave like a totally normal person and be able to stand beside a smoking hot man and not internally combust?

Because I sure as hell do not know.

Reid's hand rises to pet the kitten, and all I can do is stare. The kitten's eyes close as she begins to purr loudly, the sound rivaling a Harley Davidson, and the jealousy that flies through me at her pleasure is wholly unreasonable.

Reid chuckles. "She's a cute little thing."

"So it's settled then!" Matty releases her into Reid's hands. "I'll be right back with your supplies."

I watch him retreat before finally swinging my gaze to Reid's. "He's...pushy."

The kitten snuggles into Reid's chest and blinks at me, satisfied as hell.

Yeah, well, must be nice...

Matty returns with everything needed to take care of a kitten: wet and dry food, bowls, litter, and a litter box, along with a bottle of tiny pills for her leg. "Here we go!" he declares cheerily. "Sure is lucky that I keep these things in my trunk. I'm sure you two can determine the best way to co-parent this little baby."

"Co-parent?" I choke the word out. "What?"

But Matty's already backing away with a shit-eating grin on his face. I'm going to kill him. "It'll be great. And listen, if you two really can't figure it out—but you're both grown adults, so I'm sure you will—then I'll find another home for the sweet, helpless kitten who was wandering around the pier, hurt and about to die. It's fine."

I growl. "Is this how you do it?"

Matty holds his hand up to his ear. "Sorry, can't hear you. Gotta go. Bye!"

And with that, he's out. Skedaddled like a coward after dropping a live animal into my care.

Well. Scratch that. Into our care. In fact, not *our* care—Reid's care.

Before I can think too hard about it, I flee inside my house and slam the door.

There.

I'm like an ostrich. If I can't see him and the kitten, then they're not my problem.

A knock sounds at the door. "Willa."

"Willa's not here!" I call.

A low rumble of a laugh comes from outside, and it does things to my lower belly that it shouldn't. "Pretty sure she is."

"Nope!"

"Well, I have a little midnight-black kitten here that is rather desperate for some attention."

I huff. That kitten is already living a better life with Reid than I ever will. Screw that creature.

Honestly.

"You'll do great with her, Reid," I call.

"*We'll* do great with her," he corrects. "Because all I did was wander over here to see what the commotion was."

"That's what you get for being nosy," I chide. "Maybe you'll learn your lesson."

"Willa."

"Reid."

"I can see you through the curtains, you know."

"You mean the kitchen curtains, where you leer at me like some pervert when all I want to do is get the diner smell off me? Do you have any idea what it's like to be the walking embodiment of beef and cheese?"

He snorts a laugh. "Did you just reference *Elf*?"

"Best holiday movie there is," I state.

"Untrue. Great movie, but not the best."

"Don't come at me with your lies, Reid. *Elf* is the best, and I won't hear otherwise."

"It's *Die Hard*."

I roll my eyes. "Of course you'd think that."

"What's that supposed to mean?"

"You're a cop, Reid. Isn't it your sacred duty to think *Die Hard* is the better holiday movie—despite literally nothing happening in it that's holiday-related other than it happens to take place during the holidays? I mean, listen, Alan Rickman is the superior villain, don't get me wrong, but that is no more a holiday movie than the sun is blue."

A beat passes. "We're getting off track."

"I really shouldn't be trusted with a kitten. I can't even be trusted with a conversation."

Another soft snicker comes from Reid's side of the door. "How about…Willa, seriously. Will you open the damn door?"

"Fine." I fling it open and nearly lose my breath. Because he's standing there, all Hottie McHotFace bit of him, with a tiny baby kitten cradled in his arms, and it hits a deep part of me I do not want to think about.

He smiles. "Thank you."

I cross my arms. "You're not welcome."

His gaze flits down to my breasts before meeting my eyes again. And honestly, I should be all righteous about it and demand he keep his ogling to himself, but apparently my feminism has packed its bags because I could not be happier about him looking at my tits.

I might push my shoulders back a little.

Might.

I'm neither confirming nor denying.

"Tell you what," Reid says. "Let's do what Matty said."

"Co-parent?" I squeak, then wince. Christ on a cracker with the freaking squeaks.

He grimaces, and even *that* looks attractive on him. "Co-parent is a strong word. How about we simply both take care of the little girl until we can sort something else out?"

"And how do you propose we…share responsibility?"

"I'll take care of her when you're working, and you'll take care of her the rest of the time."

I sniff. "Doesn't sound like it's very fifty-fifty."

Reid fights a smile. "Good thing it's not a real kid we're worried about."

"Ugh, *fine.*" I stomp past him and grab all the supplies that

Matty left unceremoniously on the ground in front of my cottage and bring them inside. Then I return and hold my hands out for the kitten.

Reid hesitates. "Are we going to talk about —"

"Kitten," I cut him off.

He nods, then gingerly hands the fuzzball to me with a sigh.

I nestle her in one arm, refusing to think about how she was just in Reid's arms and now she's in mine and so it's sort of like we just hugged but not really, and retreat into my house. "Good night, Reid."

He quirks a smile. "It's four in the afternoon."

I shut the door in his face.

"I'll be sure to be inside for your daily porch-sitting session!" he calls brightly.

The kitten issues a loud yowl.

I hang my head. I am, officially, an idiot.

CHAPTER 9

REID

I FINISH THE morning's exercises for my shoulder—which is all but one hundred percent healed—then go through my pre-run stretches. I open the door ready to roll, and nearly trample Willa Dean Dash.

"Good lord, Willa!" I reel back from the doorway even as I do my customary scan of the street, and she takes a few paces backward. Together, we put about five feet between us, and immediately I hate it. I want to be closer to her.

"Kitten," she says, holding the little thing up and toward me.

"Running," I respond in kind, gesturing at my shoes.

"I've got to go to work, Reid. It's your turn. She's eaten and gone to the bathroom. You should be good." She stands with the kitten outstretched, three paws and one bandaged leg hanging in the air, little belly pooching out, blue eyes blinking as though I'm supposed to know what to do with her.

Guess I'm in charge of a kitten.

I step closer and clock how Willa stiffens a little. *There she is, my little skittish beauty.* I lower my voice. "Willa."

She flushes. "Here."

I barely get another step in before she's shoving the kitten at me and backing away again. I laugh and take the fluff ball, cuddling it against my chest with one hand. "Do I stink? Is that why you're staying so far away?"

Her cheeks grow even brighter as she shoves her hands into her khaki pants. "No," she mutters, then looks away. "I've gotta go."

I watch her flee and wish, for what seems like the millionth time, that she'd stop running away from me. Because I'd love to recreate that kiss.

But apparently, I have a kitten to deal with.

I sort out a little space for her in my living room, then ask her nicely to please behave while I head out on a run.

An hour later, I roll into the station with Midnight. Because that's what I'm calling her, and if Willa doesn't like it, she can come up with something. But I can't have a pet and her not have a name.

Not that she's *my* pet.

But still.

"Oh my word, is that a kitten?" Betty squeals, standing up from the desk and rounding it toward me. "With a bandaged leg? Oh my goodness, you poor thing," she coos, taking Midnight from me without even bothering to meet my eyes.

Well, that's one way to do it.

Betty holds the fuzzy hellion up and stares at her. "Oh, you're such a sweet little baby, aren't you?" She glances at me. "How did you come to be in possession of this preciousness?"

"Long story."

Ted Thompson struts up, thumbs hooked onto his utility belt and looking far more self-important than the situation calls for. The man raises my hackles, and I can't tell you why. But I don't like him. I can't quite tell yet if other people get the same vibe as me, but I don't know. Call it my sixth sense as a police officer. Either way, I am not fond of him.

"Can't have animals in the station," he states flatly.

Betty turns to glare at him. "Ted Thompson, you hush your mouth. It's a kitten, not some gorilla on the loose."

He looks affronted. "There are rules…"

"And if we had a police dog?" I interrupt, unwilling to let his douchery continue.

"Well, that's…that's different," he sputters.

"Is it, though?"

His ruddy complexion gets even more maroon. "No animals." He turns and leaves, and Betty rolls her eyes at his departure.

"I think he needs a hug," she says.

"He needs more than that," I mutter, keeping my voice low.

Betty laughs. "You're probably right. I've got an idea. Take this sweet thing, and I'll be right back."

I cradle Midnight against me, and moments later, Betty returns with some kind of super-long fabric.

"It's a baby sling," she declares.

"A what now?"

She gestures me toward her, then proceeds to wrap the fabric around me and secure it with a plastic loop thing that I'd not noticed before. Then she holds it open, a little pouch magically appearing in the front, and I nestle Midnight in there.

"Well, if that's not the cutest thing I've ever seen," Betty coos again.

"What the hell is going on?" Chief Mac asks as he walks in. "Are you wearing a baby?"

"She's a kitten," I correct. "Not a baby."

"Thank God. You've not been here long enough to cause that kind of trouble," Chief smiles. He reaches in and pets the kitten's head. "Cute little thing."

Midnight blinks up at me and meows, then kicks a purr into gear so loud that Chief and Betty can hear her.

Chief chuckles. "Guess you're taking her on duty?"

After only a moment's hesitation, I nod. "Pretty sure I'll fit right in." Nothing else about me in this town is normal, so why not take the next ridiculous step? I can't fathom my chief in Miami being okay with me waltzing around with a kitten strapped to my chest.

"I was gonna tell you that you were on your own today since Ox is needed for something else, but it looks like you've got a partner after all."

Betty giggles with delight. "Officer MacKinnon, you're gonna turn all the heads."

Ted grumbles from behind his desk but says nothing. I may have only been here two weeks, but even I know better than to cross the Chief *and* Betty. And the both of them have clearly given me the green light to police while cat-wearing.

My buddies in Miami would have a field day with this. Good thing they won't see me.

Of course, the whole idea of not being seen goes down the tubes when I amble into the town square. I'm swarmed by tourists, most of whom are older ladies ogling me and using the kitten as an excuse, but some are indeed there for the cat. A couple of people ask to pose near the infamous clock tower since it's got the town's name on top of it. And while part of me wonders if it's a good idea posing with Midnight for random photos with tourists, I can't imagine that it's a big deal. As cutthroat as the Bunnies are, there's no point in them worrying about anything this far north, even if it is on the coast. Nothing I learned about them in my years working undercover would lead me to believe they'd bother with a town this tiny.

My stomach growls just as I near the Dash In Diner, and Midnight pokes her head out with interest, her little whiskers quivering as she scans the front of the building.

"You wanna see your mom, little one?" I ask.

I swing open the door and am not three steps in before Goldie is cooing and darting toward me.

"Oh my gosh, is that the kitten? Aw, look at her," she says, leaning in and reaching to give her scratches. She barely spares me a glance before turning her attention back to the kitten. "I heard all about this little one and how Matty conned the two of you into co-parenting." She laughs. "You two never had a chance. Once Matty decides on a pet pairing, it's over."

"A pet pairing?" It's hard not to smile. "Well, Midnight here has enjoyed her stroll about town. She's already famous with some of the other store owners, so don't be heartbroken if one of them decides they want her."

Goldie gasps. "You would never!" Then she leans back to Midnight. "Don't listen to him. You're stuck with us, you adorable little floof. Auntie Goldie will make sure of it."

By the time I find my way to the counter, I've stopped to say hello to several locals I'm starting to recognize, and one that I definitely know.

"JJ," I intone as the man raises his camera to snap a picture.

JJ smiles happily at the digital screen, not even bothering to make eye contact now that he's gotten what he came for. "Hey, Officer."

I step closer, putting my hand on the camera and lowering it to force JJ to look at me. He blinks, his eyes wide and, dare I hope, a little scared. I lean in and drop my voice. "I'd really like it if you'd ease up on the 'new officer in town' bit. Everybody knows I'm here."

He nods, his throat bobbing. "Sure. It's just, you see, news," he says, his voice wavering. Then he gestures at Midnight. "Gotta give the town what they want, you know."

I scowl. "No, I don't know. How is this newsworthy?"

He's saved from answering when Barbara bustles over and slaps a menu on the counter. "Officer MacKinnon," she gushes.

"Just Reid," I say.

"Nonsense," she waves me off. "What are you going to order that doesn't match what's on the menu today?"

I glance at the window behind her just in time to make eye

contact with Willa. She's not glaring, and she's not flushed, so we might be making progress.

Although, if I'm being honest, riling her up is one of my favorite things to do. And I don't care how I do it: Irritate her, fluster her with a well-placed wink, or even better, kiss her senseless.

Have I mentioned how much I'd really, really like to do that again?

Midnight issues a meow to rival all meows, her tiny little kitten body flexing with the effort. I look down at her. "She's in the kitchen, girl. Can't do anything about her just yet."

I swear, the cat almost huffs.

Same, little floof. Same.

I lift a tiny paw out of the sling and wave it at Willa, who barely represses a smile before turning away to focus on the grill.

I'm waiting for Willa when she comes home later that afternoon. I call her name the second she's in my sight, and damned if that woman doesn't pretend to ignore me, *again*, and head straight for her house.

I jump up from my chair and grab Midnight from where she's been exploring at my feet. Little girl has the heart of a lion until she sees a grasshopper. Then it's game over.

"Oh, no, you don't." I jog up to Willa and lean against the doorframe, the very picture off relaxed.

She heaves a sigh. "Can't I at least—"

"No, you can't go inside and get naked." I deliberately choose the words most guaranteed to make her blush.

Sure enough, she delivers, the color rising prettily on her cheeks as she gapes at me. "Seriously?"

I smirk and hold the kitten out. "Midnight is yours now."

"I heard that's the name you gave her. Who said you got to do that?"

I shrug. "No one. And you don't have to call her that, but when she's with me, that's her name."

As anticipated, the edict riles her even more. She growls and stomps her feet, and I adore it. She's so cute when she's flustered. "Fine. Give me…Midnight."

My smile is broad as she gently takes the cat from me. "So," I start.

"Absolutely not," she answers, not remotely interested in what I was about to say.

For the record, it was going to be a suggestion that we try kissing again and see what happens.

"I'll return the cat in the morning," she says.

"Wait!"

She turns, an eyebrow raised.

"Seriously. You need her things." I hustle to my house to grab the large amount of supplies I bought at the pet store, then bring it back, ignoring the palpable sense of relief flooding my system at the fact that she actually waited on me.

Willa eyes the bag warily. "What is all that?"

"Pet supplies…from the pet supply place." I bite back a laugh. "You know, things that pets need. Food, toys, a litter box, that sort of thing."

She sniffs. "Matty gave all that to us yesterday."

"He did, but litter boxes and litter have gotten way fancier than the basic stuff he unloaded yesterday," I counter. I may have done some reading. Okay, a lot of reading. Midnight deserves the best, and if I'm being honest, I don't want my house to smell like cat pee and poo. So there's that. And if I'm getting the stuff for my house, it's only fair that I get it for Willa's too.

She sighs and holds her hand out, and I step forward. "I could bring it inside, you know."

An entire range of emotions fly over her face: surprise, desire, confusion, resignation. Finally, she shakes her head. "No. Thank you."

I fight the disappointment and nod, waiting until she's inside the house before retreating to my backyard and picking my guitar up.

And wouldn't you know it? I miss that furry terror all night.

CHAPTER 10

WILLA

THREE DAYS. THREE days of being a kitten co-parent and I am entirely over it.

Because Midnight prefers Reid over me.

And I might be jealous about it.

Is it stupid? Yes. Am I being petty? Also, yes. But the way she purrs when she gets into his hands, loudly and far too contentedly for her own good, is a bit much.

But I'd be purring if Reid's hands were all over me, too. I get it.

I work a shorter shift than usual so that Goldie and I can go to the fair that's swung into town. She pulled off a classic kid move with our parents, wheedling and whining and dropping hints for at least a week leading up to today. She acted all surprised when Mom and Dad shoved us out the door after the lunch crowd, but I'd been fully prepared.

After a quick shower and stern instructions from Goldie to once again wear the shorts from the art walk and "a cute top, so help me God," my sister picked me up, and we headed to the fair. It's stifling hot outside, but even the temperature doesn't do a thing to ruin it for me.

I inhale deeply as we pay for our tickets and enter. Scents of fried deliciousness and sounds of happy kids come at me from all directions. "I love the fair."

Goldie threads her arm through mine. "Me, too. You remember the first time Mom and Dad let us come by ourselves?"

I snort a laugh, the memory appearing immediately. "When Bobby Sharma tried to kiss you on the roller coaster and you puked? How could I not?"

She cackles. "Served Bobby right. First of all, he didn't ask permission, and second, we were on a freaking roller coaster!"

That was the last time I rode a roller coaster at the fair. I'd been lucky enough to be three rows ahead of her, so I didn't get splattered or anything gross like that, but it still ruined me for those particular kinds of rides. Besides, after realizing how often they get taken down and put back up again, and understanding that it's done over and over by mere humans who might be having a bad day or might be distracted when they do it...no thank you. If it's my life on the line, I'll stick to the rides with the least risk of death involved.

"I need funnel cake, stat," Goldie declares after we stop laughing our butts off.

So funnel cake it is. We wait in a small line, and when we get the cake, it's hot from the fryer, the powdered sugar sticking to our fingers as we eat it. Honestly, is there anything better?

I sigh happily, licking my fingers before diving for another bite, tearing off a piece, and dipping in the extra sugar piled everywhere on the paper plate. "This is the best, Goldie."

She leans into me, a smile on her face. "The best," she agrees.

An hour later, we're in a line for the Ferris Wheel. It's the only ride I'm willing to go on, and, apparently, a lot of other people agree with me.

"Oh, look," Goldie says innocently, then points. "It's Matty and Reid!"

I stiffen. Reid? Is *here*? My heart kicks into gear and I try to not be obvious as I look at my outfit. Do I have powdered sugar all over me? Doesn't look like it. But it's too late to ask Goldie because they're at our sides in seconds.

"Hi, Matty," Goldie breathes. "Hi, Reid."

I eye her. She's not spoken about Reid any more, other than in passing and to ask about the cat. But the way she just said Matty's name is new. I make a note to ask her about that later.

"It's the Dash women," Matty says happily, leaning in to give us both a hug. "Fancy seeing you here."

Is it, though? I study Goldie before turning to Reid. "Where's Midnight?"

"Home. Figured he couldn't do too much damage if I left her in the kitchen."

Matty jumps in. "I went over to check on her and convinced Reid to come to the fair. Turns out, he'd never been to a small-town fair. Obviously, I had to change that."

"Obviously," Goldie says, her eyes firmly on Matty.

"How is she?" I ask Matty.

"Ask him yourself," Matty jokes.

I swat at him. "You're the vet. How is our—*the*—cat?"

He points a finger at me. "I heard that. We all heard that. You called the kitten 'our'." He turns to Reid. "Did you hear it?"

Reid bites back a smile. "I most definitely heard it."

"And as an officer of the law, surely that means it's a binding agreement," Matty continues.

"No!" I protest weakly. "Just, come on. How's her leg? Even though if you're checking her leg, it should be at your office with the right equipment," I huff.

"Ooh, is someone concerned about the kitten she's co-parenting?" Matty teases.

I cross my arms and shuffle forward as we get closer to the front. "Whatever."

Matty chuckles. "She's doing good. Healing very quickly, just as a little kitten should. You and Reid are great pet parents."

When we're almost at the front of the line, Matty turns dramatically to Goldie. "Oh no," he pouts, his voice far too loud, "I've lost my tickets." He makes a show of looking for them.

"Oh no," Goldie says, catching on quickly.

"Then we'll step out of line," I offer, making to leave.

Goldie grabs my hand in an iron grip. "Nope. You two can go. Reid's never seen Lucky from the air, right?"

Reid, the bastard, is more than happy to go along with this farce. "Why no, Goldie, I haven't. Tell me, is it a good view?"

She nods vigorously. "The best. Here." She pulls the tickets out of her pocket and shoves them at Reid. "Take mine. Matty and I will—"

"Leave," Matty finishes, stepping out of line and smiling at me mischievously.

I flatten my lips, fully aware of what they've all conspired to do. Then I try to breathe. Because the prospect of being alone again with Reid, *really* alone with him, no purring kitten between us, is a little daunting.

Scratch that. It's terrifying. Nauseating. Exciting. Confusing.

Matty and Goldie take off, cackling like they've gotten away with the best ruse on the planet, and Reid looks down at me as they drift out of sight. "You okay?"

I lick my lips and nod. "I'm fine."

He hands our tickets to the guy at the front, who waves us in, bored and distracted by his phone. A couple gets off the seat in front of us, and the second worker gestures for us.

"Ladies first," Reid says, holding his hand out to steady me as I step up and onto the swinging bench.

In seconds, we're side by side on the bench and the worker has snapped the bar over us, wiggling it to make sure it's locked, and stepping away.

The ride lurches into action, and I grip the bar tightly, emitting a tiny *eep* as we immediately come to another stop.

"Are you okay?" Reid's voice is full of concern. "It's not too late —"

"I'm fine," I repeat.

"Are you afraid of heights or something? Because seriously, Willa—"

I shake my head. "That's not it. Heights are fine." We lurch into movement again, this time going up a few chairs' worth of spaces into the air. My heart is beating a billion miles an hour, and all I can think is how I'm going to throttle Matty and Goldie if I make it off here in one piece.

Reid touches my hand. "Not sure the death grip is doing you any favors."

I whimper. I can't sort my emotions fast enough.

"You know," he says conversationally, draping his arm around the back of the chair and settling into the ride, "Seems like those two want us to get together. Same for Agatha."

I look at him. "I, uh..." I stammer. What do I say to that? "Um. Yeah? I guess so?"

He turns his attention to me, and he's even better looking in this light than normal, the way the faded sunset cedes to the neon lights of the Ferris Wheel. "Would that be so bad?"

I blink. "You're not serious."

He wraps his arm around me and pulls me closer. We've moved farther up now, near the top. Behind us, the ocean stretches into the distance, and neon lights blur the scene all around us. Reid smells so good. This is going to be my undoing. *Breathe.*

"I'm serious, Willa." He tilts his head down and cups my chin, forcing me to look into his eyes. They're a deep green in this light, the darkest parts of a forest. And I'm the girl lost in them. "I'm going to kiss you now."

I squeak.

He smiles gently. "Please?"

I bite my lip and nod. When I finally find my voice and speak, it comes out as a strangled whisper. "Okay."

His lips meet mine for the second time in my life, and it's just as life-altering as the first kiss. The scruff of his days-old beard scrapes against my lips, rough and unyielding, and my body thrills to have it. Instinct takes over. I open my mouth on a moan, and he pulls me tighter, closing the distance between us on the bench. His tongue explores my mouth, softly, almost sweetly, but I can feel the coiled tension behind it, as though if he was given enough time, he'd have me laid out. There's no questioning the desire he has for me. I feel it in the way his breath hitches when I reach up to thread my fingers through his hair. The way he makes me feel is terrifying. He's the Tilt-a-Whirl I refuse to go on because I know I won't survive, and yet, I can't stop.

"You're scary." I blurt the words the second we part, my lips still tingling from his kiss.

He laughs, still cradling my face. "How am *I* scary?"

"Because you're *you.*"

"What does that mean, I'm me?" he presses, his hand warm against my skin.

"Just...you're *you*. Sophisticated and gorgeous and funny and clearly the better kitten parent." I say the last part with no amount of jealousy.

Okay, it's a ton of jealousy.

His smile broadens, and he holds me in place as he kisses me again. His lips are heartbreakingly gentle and soft as they move over mine, sipping at me like I'm a bottle of the finest wine.

It feels too intimate, too real. I pull myself away and look over the town. "Isn't it beautiful?"

"Yes." But his eyes are firmly on me as he speaks. It doesn't take a genius to know he's not talking about the view. He threads his fingers through my hair, and even though the rational part of me insists on all of this stopping immediately, I can't help but close my eyes and hum with pleasure.

"Is this what Midnight feels every time you touch him? No wonder you're the better parent."

His fingers don't stop. "Willa. Let me take you out. For a real date." He pauses. "Though I do like this—you can't run away from me here."

My cheeks heat. "I don't know how to act around you. I told you, you're scary."

His eyes soften, their green hue suddenly beyond vibrant as we move quickly through the bottom and come to a halt halfway up for a second rotation. "I am the farthest thing from scary, Willa."

I snort. "Lies."

He runs a finger from the top of my forehead down the slope of my nose, then to my lips and chin. "I don't want to scare you. I want to take you on a date." He grins. "There's a big difference."

How does this man, this gorgeous man with more muscles than I can fathom, want to go on a date with me? None of it makes sense. I'm the girl who no one ever wanted to date in school. Who relied almost exclusively on tourists to get any sort of experience growing up. Who even now couldn't catch a guy's interest if my life depended on it. Yet here's the most unbelievably good-looking man on the freaking planet, sitting in a tiny metal seat on a Ferris Wheel with me, kissing me and asking me out.

Reid smiles again, this time popping a dimple, and I sigh. "You're doing that on purpose."

He widens his eyes innocently. "Me? Doing what?"

I shove at his chest, and he captures it there, flattening my palm against a pec muscle. Holy crap, it's so freaking firm. I'd pass out if I ever got a look at his chest. His hand is warm. His smile is sincere. His eyes…they'll be the death of me, all twinkly and gorgeous and fracturing my resolve with every passing minute.

"Say yes, Willa."

And it's stupid, because I know that whatever this is, it won't go anywhere, but I nod. "Yes."

Then he kisses me again, and I don't bother fighting the butterflies that launch inside my belly.

After three rotations, we get off the Ferris Wheel. Reid reaches for my hand, linking our fingers together and leading me to where Matty and Goldie wait on us.

Goldie looks at our joined hands and meets my eyes, smiling broadly. "How was the ride?"

"You know how it was," I say, not willing to let her off the hook.

Matty laughs. "It's weird. Once you guys got on the ride, I found my tickets."

"So weird," I deadpan.

"Anyway," Goldie drawls, brandishing the fair's schedule on her phone, "there's a banana derby happening in fifteen minutes, so you know what I want to do."

Reid glances down at me, then the others. "A banana derby?"

"Where monkeys wear tiny jockey outfits to ride dogs and they race," Matty supplies, seeing the confusion on Reid's face. "Probably not fancy enough for a city boy like you to have experienced."

Reid laughs delightedly. "Oh, I am in. Lead me to the monkeys."

"I should note that this particular fair has been certified as treating the monkeys and dogs well," Matty points out. "Last year, I even did an annual exam on all of them when the fair was here."

"Of course you did," I smile. "Your bleeding heart would have run them out of town if it were any other way."

"It's our duty to speak for those who can't speak for themselves," he says. "And on that note, let's go watch ourselves a race!"

We spend hours at the fair. The banana derby is funny and

cute, as always, but watching Reid see it for the first time is absolutely one of my new favorite things. I can see the little kid he must have been, in the way his eyes glitter with excitement and pure joy, because again, monkeys are riding dogs around a little track in a race, and how is that not the best thing ever?

We wait in line for Reid to get a picture with the winning monkey, and he then proceeds to absolutely crush Matty in the games tent. Matty protests the unfairness of the water-gun balloon race, but after Reid lets him pick the stuffed animal to take as his own prize, he relents. "Fine. You're a better shot than me."

Reid laughs. "I'm a cop, man. If I weren't a better shot than a veterinarian, I'd be ashamed of myself."

"Yeah, well, I'm a better shot-giver, so there's that," Matty grumbles.

I hand Matty some cotton candy. "Of course you are," I soothe. "No one's a better shot-giver than you, boo."

At the end of the night, we walk to our cars. As I head to Goldie's, she shakes her head. "Why don't you ride with Reid?"

Reid tugs me back, a sexy grin on his face. "Yeah. Ride home with me, Willa." His voice is low and darkly promising.

I shiver, unwilling to investigate whether it's the night air or Reid that has me covered in goosebumps. One look at Goldie's expression, then at Reid's, has me once again going against my own best interests. "Okay."

We say our goodbyes, and Reid opens the truck door to help me in. The cab smells like him, hints of cedar and honey comforting me as he rounds the front and gets in, smiling at me and sending the butterflies into a tizzy once more.

"You have got to stop doing that," I admonish.

"Doing what?" He starts the engine.

"Smiling."

He gives a full-on belly laugh, free and unencumbered, and it's like listening to angels singing. It makes me giddy.

We're quiet on the drive home, mainly because I can't think of anything to say. Even giving him crap about Midnight isn't something I want to do. I study his profile as he drives. His hair, a little longer than I suspect he prefers it, is pushed away from his face in dark waves, and his nose is strong and straight. His skin is naturally tan, and his cheekbones are high, all the better to show off those dimples when he smiles. His lips are full, and they part now in a sensual grin as he turns to me. "You're staring, Willa."

My blood heats, and at this point, I'm fairly certain that my entire body is blushing.

"If it makes you feel any better," he continues, not waiting on me to answer him, "I stare at you every chance I get, too."

I have no idea what to say to that, but now my blood is boiling.

I try to tamp it down—he's a flirt, and he's only here for three months—but it's hard. Because when was the last time a guy gave me this kind of attention?

Never. The answer is never.

He pulls into his driveway and kills the engine, then hops out and is opening my door before I can get it myself. He holds his hand out, and even though I'm perfectly capable of getting down from his ridiculously high truck, I take it. It's strong and warm, gentle, and calloused. I meet his eyes when my feet hit the ground. "Thank you for tonight."

He studies me. "Anytime." Weaving our fingers together once again, he leads me not to his house like I was kind of hoping, but down Agatha's driveway and around to my cottage. His jaw ticks as he surveys the property. "You should have your porch light on."

I grin. "It's safe back here, Officer MacKinnon."

"Come here." Reid's voice is as dark as the night, silky and full of promise.

Despite everything, I go to him willingly, letting him gather me into his arms and pull me tight. This time, when he leans down to kiss me, I'm ready for it. And I refuse to be the one to break it, because if I'm being honest with myself, I'd like to continue the kissing inside my house. Perhaps with fewer clothes.

Actually, that would definitely be my preference. His house, my house, I don't care: just fewer clothes, please.

His hands roam my body, sending streaks of pleasure through me as they map my rear, hips, waist, and stomach. He stops when his palms are right below my breasts, and his thumbs trace the underside of them through my bra.

I hitch in a breath and arch my back in silent invitation. *Yes, please.*

But he doesn't go farther. Instead, he eases up on the kiss, and even though I don't want to, I follow his lead, relinquishing the hold I have on him.

"You don't have to stop, you know," I breathe, giving voice to my desire.

He kisses my cheek. "Yeah, Willa, I do."

"Really, you don't."

He kisses my other cheek, then steps back. "Really, I do. Goodnight, Willa Dean Dash."

I roll my eyes even as my heart skips a beat. "Just Willa."

He smirks, popping a dimple. "Goodnight, Just Willa."

He waits for me to go inside, and I hear his next words through the door. "Lock the door."

I do as he asks, then pull the curtain to watch him walk away. The man has an incredible butt.

Later, after I'm tucked into bed, I get a text from Reid. It's a picture of Midnight on a pillow, curled up like a little fuzzy black ball on what must be Reid's bed. Then, another text comes in behind it.

REID

Midnight says goodnight.

More dots pop up, and in moments, I have a third text.

I'd prefer you to be on this pillow.

I squeal, kicking the covers and squirming. How is this real life? How? Just...*how?*

I heart the picture of Midnight and type back.

Goodnight, Reid.

REID

Goodnight, Just Willa.

REID

UNCLE JACK CALLS me into his office on Saturday morning. I've been in town and on the job for three weeks now, and I've been expecting an update from Miami. He waves me to close the door and have a seat, which I do. Then he puts the phone on speaker. "Muñoz? I've got him."

"Hey, Chief."

"MacKinnon," comes Chief Muñoz's voice, booming and strong as always. "How's Lucky treating you?"

"Good. Quiet," I answer. "It's a nice change of pace."

He laughs. "I bet."

"You got news?" May as well get to it.

"DA says we have enough evidence to charge your contacts in the Bunnies. We got one in custody still, and plan on grabbing the other two this week. DA thinks it's enough to put them away. It's a big step, MacKinnon. We wouldn't be here without the work you did."

I nod, meeting my uncle's eyes. "Thanks, Chief."

"How's your recovery?"

"Good."

"Doing your physical therapy?"

I chuckle. "Every morning before my run."

"Excellent. We want you at 100 percent when you get back. You're missed around here."

I startle. I don't know that the man has ever said anything so…emotional. "Sure thing."

We hang up, and my uncle regards me, stroking his mustache and studying what feels like every inch of me. When I'm nearly ready to squirm, he finally speaks. "You know, you have a job here if you want it."

I open my mouth to tell him no, but something stops me. Which is ridiculous. But what's not ridiculous is the way images of Willa flit unbidden across my mind. A woman I am definitely interested in, and a woman who absolutely will not be heading back to Miami with me—no matter what her friends and family might want to happen. I may have only known her for a couple of weeks, but it's clear to me she won't leave this town. And I wouldn't ask her to.

At the same time, what kind of life would I have here? It's so…slow. After spending the last few years undercover, in a pretty constant state of anxiety, if I'm being honest, my body still doesn't know how to take all of this…stillness. Despite the town's hazing, which has been nothing short of charming in a way, my time here has almost felt like a vacation.

"Think about it," Jack says, sensing that I don't really have anything to say about it. "And take the day off."

"It's Saturday," I protest. "Don't I need to go write at least fifty licensing citations to the people on the pier?"

He laughs. "You know you don't."

"Yeah, that's Thompson's gig," I smirk. The man gets far too much enjoyment out of issuing those things. He's also the exact kind of asshole cop who tickets people for the ticky-tacky things they usually don't even know about, like burned-out rear lights. I'm about to insist on doing the shift, but then he says, "Willa's off today."

Dammit. My eyes fly to his, and they straight-up twinkle. I bet he'd make a great Santa if he let his beard grow.

He laughs and shoos me out the door. "Thought so. Go. Enjoy the day. I'm not always this generous."

I leave before he changes his mind, swinging past the Piggly Wiggly to grab some wet food and a toy for Midnight as my excuse for the visit. Then I head home to change out of my uniform, putting my gun in the safe and making sure it's locked before leaving through the back and closing the distance to Willa's.

She answers the door, and I nearly swallow my tongue. She's in a dark blue, silky pajama set. Her hair is tousled and she absolutely, with no question, is not wearing a bra. She holds Midnight against her chest, her lips bare, and she blinks up at me.

Lord, give me strength. I have never prayed for help in the face of unbound breasts, but I think now is a grand time to start. How, *how*, am I supposed to resist this woman?

"Reid!" Her voice comes out high-pitched and tinny, and she winces. She clears her throat, the pink I adore already blooming across her cheeks, and tries again. "H-hi," she stammers. "What's up? I mean, why are you here?"

I fall back on the dimpled smile that's guaranteed to increase her blush. "I brought treats." I hold up the plastic bag and hoping she doesn't notice the way my pants have gotten just a little tighter around the crotch area. Midnight mewls pitifully, scrabbling to get out of Willa's hands and into mine like some sort of baby who's seen her favorite uncle.

Willa rolls her eyes at the kitten's antics but hands her over and takes the bag out of my grip. With a shy smile, she says, "Come on in, then."

It's the first time I've been in here. The kitchen is small but clearly used, the counters stuffed with cooking implements and spices. She sets the bag down on the table, and I follow her to the living room. She gestures for me to have a seat on the couch, but

I'm too busy looking at the incredible amounts of doilies scattered about.

"Willa. Are you a secret doily maker?" I ask, half afraid of the answer.

She crosses her arms. "No. They came with the place."

I choke out a laugh. "And you've kept them on display? There's…" I trail off to count. "At least ten in here."

"I'm well aware."

"Doilies for cups, doilies for the arms of the couch, doilies for …"

She cuts me off. "I know. They're not so bad."

"Willa. They're *so* bad." I choke out a laugh.

Willa widens her eyes and gestures to Agatha's house. "Well, what am I supposed to tell her? 'Sorry, Agatha, I can't keep these on display in my house because they're a crime against the twenty-first century'?"

I laugh. "That is precisely what you should tell her."

"Yeah, you try telling her that and see how far you get."

"You're right," I say after a moment of consideration. "It's a terrible idea."

She laughs and points at me. "Exactly."

Midnight mewls in my arms, and it's only then that I realize I've been holding her this whole time. I nod to the bag she left in the kitchen. "I brought a toy and some treats. Wanna give them to her?"

She hums and turns away, and because I'm an asshole, I take the opportunity to watch her walk away from me. Christ. Those tiny shorts might be the death of me. She returns with the toys: A plush mouse with some catnip inside it and a little stick with feathers on it. I put the kitten down, and she immediately pounces on the mouse.

I laugh. "Guess she likes it."

"She's a cat. Pretty sure it's in her DNA." Then she pauses. "Do you…wanna stay for a while? Hang out?"

"Yes." I can't say it fast enough, and I don't care if it makes me seem like an eager schoolboy. I want to hang out with her. I want to know so much more about her. And if that means I sound over-eager, then so be it.

Smiling, she sits on one end of the couch and I take the other, trying hard not to ogle the way she curls her legs beneath her, and trying even harder not to wonder if she's wearing panties under those shorts. It's clear she had no intentions of a visitor today. What's amazing is that she hasn't bothered to change out of her pajamas or even brush her hair. Is this what she would be like if we woke up together? Only, of course, she'd be naked, those silk pajamas a distant memory as I ran my fingers over her sk—

"Reid?"

I snap out of it. "Hmm?"

"I asked if I could get you something. Water? Coffee? It's no Dash In Diner coffee, but it'll do the trick." She smiles again, and it's radiant. Innocent.

I really am an asshole. But in my defense, I *did* stop myself from mauling her last night. "Um, coffee is great. Thank you."

She gets up again, and I follow her back to the tiny but serviceable kitchen. "Do you cook in here?"

She grimaces. "Is it bad if I say barely?"

"No," I laugh. "But there's a lot in here."

"I have dreams of owning a house big enough to have a huge kitchen. Like, I don't need to have the latest gadgets or anything, but an electric stove?" She shivers in the direction of the offending appliance. "Ew." Then she hands me the coffee. "You take it black, right?"

I lift the cup in a cheer. "Like my soul."

"I don't know. You seem pretty nice to me, Reid." The compliment is like an arrow to my heart, and I shouldn't feel the thrill that rises fast and hard at that small compliment.

"I thought I was scary," I smirk.

She blushes, shyly admitting, "You're both. You're…" She trails off.

"Oh, no," I tease. "You can't stop there. I am positive that you were about to give me a *ton* of compliments, and I'm just shallow enough to want to hear them. Keep going." I take a sip of coffee and gesture her to speak.

She turns away from me, stretching to open a cabinet and pulling out a cup, then filling it with water from the sink. Turning and leaning against the counter, she regards me. "I'm sure you've heard it all."

I shake my head. "Nope. I've heard nothing. I insist you pile all the compliments on me."

She laughs, and I want to make her do that again and again. "Fine. You seem very nice—"

"I *am* very nice," I correct her.

She giggles and rolls her eyes. "And smart and funny."

"You forgot handsome."

She blushes. "And handsome."

I want to kiss her so badly. But I also want to keep talking to her, and I have a feeling that I can't have both. If I kiss her now, she might kick me out.

My stomach picks this time to gurgle.

"And hungry. Handsome and hungry," she laughs.

Shrugging a little sheepishly, I say, "I'm nearly always hungry. My mom had a hell of a time keeping enough food in the house when I was growing up."

"Yeah?" It's an invitation to tell her more.

"Yeah. Standard stuff. I was an active kid, grew like a weed, played baseball like I was going to be the next MLB player, the normal kid stuff."

"That sounds nice."

I take another sip of coffee. "It was."

"Any brothers or sisters?"

"Only child. Parents divorced, but nothing traumatic, you

know? Mom cleaned hotels and eventually worked up to a manager role, and she still does that now. Dad owns a cell-phone repair shop. He remarried pretty quickly—I don't think he was made to be single," I laugh. "He's fairly helpless."

"I can't imagine my dad being helpless. That's so far outside the realm of possibility that I can't fathom it."

"Your parents are good people."

She nods and smiles softly. "Yeah. They are. So, you want lunch?"

I hesitate.

"I mean, I'll make you something," she clarifies. Then she grins. "Only, you can't be a pain in the butt about it and try to piss me off."

I chuckle. "Willa, you know I only do it to get a rise out of you."

She blushes. "No, you don't."

"I absolutely do."

She blinks rapidly, then clears her throat and opens the fridge, breaking eye contact. Behind the door, she says, "So. Lunch?"

"Definitely."

She rustles in the refrigerator, then straightens. "You allergic to anything?"

"What if I say sesame seeds?"

She glares. "Reid."

I laugh and hold up my hands. "I'm joking. No allergies. Can I help?"

"No, just stand there and look pretty." She shoots the words out, then her cheeks blaze again as I guffaw.

"Did you just call me pretty?" I tease.

"Forget I said that and I'll let you stay in here."

"Already forgotten." The way she's wearing no bra, and how her shorts ride up every time she bends into the fridge, however? Definitely not forgetting that. Ever. The image of her, pure and sweet and making me lunch, will be burned into my memory forever.

I am the Big Bad Wolf, and she's Red Riding Hood, all innocent and ready to ply me with food. Asshole that I am, I'm perfectly happy to be the wolf. Maybe she'll even let me eat her later.

She moves with efficiency around the tiny kitchen, her movements sharp and practiced. In no time, she's prepared us grilled cheese and tomato chutney sandwiches alongside an arugula salad with cranberries and sliced parmesan. It's deceptively simple, and easily the best meal I've ever had. I groan as I try, and fail, not to shovel the sandwich in my mouth like a…well, wolf. "Willa. Seriously?"

She stops, her fork halfway to her mouth. "What? Is the arugula bad?"

"This is unreal. It's delicious."

She relaxes, her eyes shining and a shyly confident smile playing around her mouth. "I know. You're welcome."

I smirk. "So *this* is where you flex, huh?"

"What do you mean?" she asks, picking up her sandwich.

I remind myself to swallow before talking. I really was raised with manners, despite how I'm inhaling this food. "I mean, you act all sweet and nice, but then you get in the kitchen and watch out. You're a beast. No wonder everyone wants you out of Lucky." When she startles and looks away, her shoulders rising, I realize what a sore spot I've poked. "Shit. I'm sorry. I get it, Willa, you're not going anywhere."

"I know I'm sheltered—"

"I didn't say that."

"Reid."

I snap my mouth shut.

"Like I said, I know I'm sheltered, but…is that really a bad thing?" Her voice rises as she talks. "If sheltered means surrounded by the people you love in the place you call home, then I'll take it every day of the week." She looks away. "Sorry. It's just…Sorry," she says again.

"Don't ever apologize for standing up for yourself, Willa. Especially with me."

She bites her lip, then nods wordlessly.

I continue. "I only meant that you're…" Sexy. Funny. One of a kind. "Amazing. Your food is incredible. I mean, I can cook, but you can *cook*."

"No. You can cook." She glares at me. "You're an asshole about it, actually."

"Wait. What?" My jaw unhinges.

After wiping her mouth and setting the cloth napkin beside her plate, she continues, "Where do you get off being so good at it? It's beyond irritating."

I laugh. "My mom wasn't about to let me not know how to cook. Besides, for a lot of years there, the only way either of us was going to get a good meal was if I cooked it. She worked hard and got home late more often than not. I had to learn."

She nods appreciatively. "I get that. Only did you have to be *that* good?"

"You afraid of a little competition?" I joke.

She harrumphs. "No. Not even a little. But I'm still pissed about that pork you made."

"Took me a year to perfect that dish, but once I did?" I kiss my fingers and preen.

"Yeah, yeah," she grumbles.

I wink. "Maybe if you're good, I'll teach you."

Her eyes flash and cheeks flush as the realization of what I said hits me. Fire crackles along the back of my neck.

I ball the cloth napkin in my hand and stand, the chair scraping against the floor.

"I'll get that," she says, grabbing for the plates.

"Absolutely not. You cooked, I clean. That's the rule."

"But—"

"But nothing. You'll stand there, and you'll take it." I growl the words, and immediately want to take them back. First I tell her I'm going to teach her if she's good, and now I tell her she'll stand there and take it?

Worried that I've crossed a line, I look over from where I've started the water at the sink. She's staring at me, and maybe I've thrown her for a loop, but overall, I don't think she's glitching. I smirk. "You good?"

She clears her throat. "Right. Sure. So, ah, tell me about why you're here. You got shot, right?"

I wince. "Wow, going straight for it, aren't you?"

"Oh, you don't have to talk about it if you don't want to," she says, immediately backtracking.

I scrub the pan. "It's okay." I'm not about to tell her about the Bunnies. She really is sheltered, and she's far too innocent and precious to get caught up in even the story of them. "Just a traffic stop gone wrong. I needed a break from Miami, and when my uncle Jack suggested I come here to fill in for Jessica, my chief was good with it, and it seemed like a great idea." I glance over at her as I finish my lie, ignoring the twinge of guilt. I was undercover for years, so the lying shouldn't make me feel as bad as it does, but there's something about this woman that makes me want to go to my knees and confess everything. All my sins, all my desires…all of which are currently about her.

And all of which are very, *very* explicit.

I finish the dishes, and we head back to the couch. We end up throwing on the Great British Baking Show and watching it for hours, with Midnight alternating between curling between us or playing with her toys.

"I could listen to him talk me to sleep every night," Willa sighs, stretching her legs and issuing the tiniest of squeals as she does it.

"The British dude talking right now?" I ask, tearing my gaze away from her luscious thighs. Then I throw on my best accent.

"Willa's chosen to bake a three-tiered Chantilly cake with a cream and cherry compote."

Willa laughs. "That's a terrible impression of him."

And finally, I can't take it anymore. I've managed to control myself all day, and frankly, I deserve a damn medal for it. It's been Olympic levels of restraint. I close the distance on the couch, the doilies on the back of the cushions framing us rather perfectly. "Willa."

She hiccups.

I smile. Even *that* is so fucking adorable. "Can I kiss you?"

Her hesitation lasts a fraction of a second. "Yes," she rasps.

"Thank fuck." On a sigh, I pull her to me.

CHAPTER 12

WILLA

REID IS KISSING me. Again. Angels are singing, and Reid is kissing me.

You'd think I'd be used to this by now. It's the third time.

I am nowhere near used to it.

No one gets used to this kind of kiss, and if they do, good for them, but that is most definitely not me.

How a man like him wants someone like me is a mystery that I will never solve. But for now, I give in to it. I let myself drown in the feel of his arms around me, the scratchy fabric of the old couch on my skin, his masculine scent, all of it overwhelming in the best way as I sigh into him.

He groans. "Willa, you're killing me."

He tastes like the lemonade I made him, tart yet sweet. He tilts my head, his hand on my chin, taking sips of me the same way he sipped the drink.

But *I'm* killing *him?* Dude. A heavy ache settles in my core, and my breasts are taut with want. "Not as much as you're killing me, Reid MacKinnon."

He sucks in a breath and pulls back, his eyes a dark emerald, blown with lust so that I can barely see the rim of his irises. "I need to taste you, Willa."

A shiver snakes through me.

He frowns. "Are you cold?"

I shake my head, another shiver wracking my body.

He pulls me on top of him with a sinful growl, my knees bracketing his hips as his strong arms encircle me once more. There's no mistaking the bulge in his jeans, and it's instinctual to rock against it.

He shifts beneath me, gently meeting my thrusts. "Fuck, Willa." His hands slip up the loose fabric of my shirt, lightly grazing my overheated skin. My eyes roll back in my head as my breath hitches, the sensation almost too much to bear.

"So silky," he murmurs, nipping at my lips before claiming them again as he wraps his hands around my breasts.

We moan together, the sound ratcheting my arousal up another notch. He runs his thumbs over my nipples, and I arch into him, lifting and pressing my hips against the fabric of his jeans.

"Jesus fucking Christ, Willa," he says, exhaling a ragged breath. "I—fuck."

"Same," I manage back. I rip my top off, clumsy as always, but so desperate for him to have as much of me as he wants that I can't be bothered to care. I claw at his shirt, whimpering. "Off. Please."

He pushes up enough for me to pull the fabric off, and then his skin is against mine, and I'm delirious because, holy cow, this man.

His lips are on my neck, hot and wet. "Fucking pajamas, Willa. All day with the pajamas," he growls, his lips traveling down as his hand snakes up to pull my hair out of its ponytail.

I throw my head back, absolutely lost to the sensation of being seduced by him. The feel of his mouth as it travels down my collarbone and stops, nipping and sucking, is next level. Who kisses like this? I understand now that I have never been kissed. Not really. Not in any way that counts.

His lips travel lower, locking onto a nipple and making me surge upward. "Oh God," I choke out.

One hand grips my ass as the other holds me against him. "Take what you want, baby," he commands, then swirls his tongue over my nipple.

I mewl, sounding far too much like Midnight for my own comfort, but I can't stop myself. Then Reid surges upright, taking me with him in a smooth motion that has me on my back on the couch and him crouching between my legs.

"Let me taste you, Willa. Can I do that?"

All I can do is stare. He's asking permission? Obviously, the answer is yes. Only I can't manage to make my voice work because when I try, all I do is squeak.

He smiles, those damn dimples popping and his eyes twinkling. "Is that a yes?"

I'm going to pass out. Just poof: Pass right the fuck out. But I keep my shit together long enough to shake my head vigorously. "Y-yes," I say, only it's more of a hoarse whisper.

He starts to slide down me.

"Wait!"

He stops and looks up.

"I need—" I scoot up, forcing him back on his haunches. "I need to see you."

His smile broadens. "Whatever you want, Willa. Take your time."

And so for one glorious minute—or five, I have no idea—I take my fill of him. He's...stunning. Darkly tanned skin that's taut with muscles upon muscles. He's fit, but not bulky. There's at least one tattoo, no, two, that deserve closer inspection when I'm not out of my head with disbelief that he's between my legs, waiting on me to give him the green light. Ignoring the bit of gauze taped over what I know must be where he was shot, I run my hands over his chest, watching his expression as I do so, trying to gauge what he might like.

"Like you mean it," he says, putting his hands over mine and pressing them onto his chest. "Touch me like you mean it."

His muscles flex beneath my touch, and when I lick my lips, his eyes follow the movement hungrily.

"Need your skin," he mutters, bending back over to kiss me. "Need every bit of your sweet taste, Willa."

He claims my mouth over and over, his hips canting into mine relentlessly, pulsing slowly, and I'm nearly out of my head with desire. "Reid," I whisper.

"Now, can I taste you?" he asks. "I want to make you feel good."

I nod, and he flashes a dazzling smile before sliding down the couch.

He rises and tucks his thumbs beneath the waist of my sleep shorts, a final question in his expression. I nod, and he peels them down, then swears. "No panties?"

"I don't wear them to bed, and then you came by, and I never..." I trail off. "Probably should have put real clothes on. Guess that was rude of me."

He rips his gaze away from where he's been transfixed and meets my eyes. "Sweetheart, it was the farthest thing from rude. It was a goddamn gift."

Then he descends, sliding most of his body off the couch to settle his face between my thighs. He breathes in, then swears again, this time more softly. "Gorgeous."

I'm holding my breath, and it's only when his lips press onto my pubic bone that it leaves me in a rush. "F-f-fuck," I choke out.

"You have no idea, Willa," he groans. "You're soaked."

"Of course I am," I retort, squirming under his inspection. "Look at you."

He huffs a laugh, the breath of it hitting my over-sensitized flesh. "No, sweetheart. It's all you." And with that, he presses his mouth to me, and I buck against him.

"Oh God, I'm sorry," I say, trying to be still.

He sucks at me lazily, his tongue swirling and licking as if he's got all the time in the world. One hand trails up my bent leg while his other gently guides me to spread for him. "Don't hold back, Willa. Don't you dare."

Well.

In that case.

Then he stops talking, all his attention focused between my legs, and I soar into the stars. His mouth is beyond talented, and I hitch in breath after breath, trying to keep my wits about me. But it's impossible. His tongue dips into me, as his thumb spreads me farther.

"Let go, sweetheart," he urges.

My hands thread into his hair as he hums against my body. He clamps onto my clit, and I jerk, moaning at the sensation. When he pushes a finger into me, I cry out. "Oh God. Oh God, ohmygod Reid." Then I'm chanting and begging him not to stop, and all I know is his mouth and his fingers.

His other hand reaches up for my breast, squeezing it almost painfully, and it's exactly what I need. All sensation swirls and locks into motion, the sweet tightening of pleasure finally releasing and tipping me into bliss. "Reid!" I yell as the orgasm takes over, and I lose control of my body, my hips bucking into his face as I ride out the most intense orgasm of my life.

Reid takes me all the way through it, never letting up, following my lead, easing up only when I collapse into the couch cushions. I blink back into real life as his lips touch the inside of my thigh, then move up to my belly.

When he gets to my mouth, he kisses me deeply, and I taste myself on him. It's hot. Far more erotic than I thought it would be. He pulls away and grins. "You, sweet Willa, look thoroughly debauched. It's a great look."

I giggle. "Thank you?" I ask. Then I yawn, and it's loud and big. I cover my mouth. "Sorry," I murmur.

He kisses my forehead. "Stay here. I'll be right back."

He returns a few moments later with a warm, wet washcloth and wipes between my legs. It's sweet and intimate, and I don't know what to do.

"Relax," he says, his voice soft and soothing.

"Mmm," is all I can say in response. I close my eyes and listen to him talk about everything and nothing.

The next thing I know, I wake up and Midnight is mewing, wanting to be let down to go to the litter box. I sit up, more than a little discombobulated and trying to figure out what's happened.

It's late. Very late. I'm covered with a blanket, and still very much naked.

My cheeks flame. Oh my God. I fell asleep after Reid MacKinnon made me come.

I am, officially, the worst.

The man gives me the best oral sex of my life—not that he had a lot of competition, but still—and I fall asleep on him.

Mortified doesn't begin to cover it.

I let Midnight out of the blanket prison she's gotten herself into, then pad into my bedroom. I put on fresh pajamas and fall into bed, snuggling into the cool sheets in the hope they relieve my overheated body.

CHAPTER 13

WILLA

Agatha is puttering in the backyard when I emerge from my house the next morning. Reid stands beside her, bare-chested, the morning sun glinting off his golden muscles. And God bless America, the man is in his standard tiny running shorts, as well. Since I've decided I'm no longer going to hide from him—there's truly no point—I take a good look at his legs.

Huh. It turns out that I might be a leg woman. It's taken me till I'm twenty-nine, ladies and gentlemen, but I am here to tell you that legs are where it's at. L-E-G-S legs.

Or maybe butts. Because his is perfectly rounded like a freaking apple or something, just begging for me to bite it.

I shake myself. What the hell is wrong with me? The man gives me a life-changing orgasm and suddenly, I turn into an objectification monster.

I shrug. You know what? I'm okay with it. The man is objectively fine. Better than fine. Drop-dead gorgeous. Adonis himself. A specimen worthy of study by the finest sculptors. What's a girl to do but enjoy it?

As if on cue, Agatha and Reid turn to me. "Good morning,

Willa," Reid says, his smile so deep his dimples pop. I could swim in those things.

My cheeks heat immediately, and my knees threaten to go weak at the sight of him. So help me if I faint. I need to eat.

Then I see the tiny bandage on his upper right shoulder, and the post-orgasmic bliss I was in gets doused. We're talking Niagara Falls levels of cold water here, and I swallow the shock of it back. I saw it yesterday, of course, but I was too busy being all lusty and such that it didn't really sink in. It's not much to look at now, but it's two distinct reminders: One, he's got a dangerous job. Two, said dangerous job is in Miami. He is not staying here.

This exact moment in time, however, is not when I get to have a crisis—existential, physical, or otherwise. So I pull myself together and toss a smile at them that would make Goldie proud. "Good morning, Reid. Good morning, Agatha."

"Join us for some coffee?" Agatha asks.

I wiggle my keys in the air. "I've got brunch duty this morning, can't."

Reid jogs over to me, his eyes roaming my body appreciatively. "Hi," he murmurs.

I squirm at the attention, despite my own ogling and full-on entry into the Objectification Hall of Fame. Between that and the reminder that he's leaving, it's hard to meet his eyes. "Hi."

He chuckles softly. "Don't make it weird, Willa."

I cover my face with my hands and groan, the memory of what *I* did after what *he* did overtaking every other thought in my head. "Kinda hard not to when I apparently passed out after you, you know." My voice drops on the last two words, as if my body is physically manifesting how embarrassed I was.

Am. How embarrassed I *am*. Ugh. Since meeting the man, I've banged my head, played a crap game of hide and seek, nearly passed out, and now we can add *fell asleep after the most intense orgasm of her life* to the list.

My awkwardness clearly knows no bounds.

Reid shifts closer and I catch his scent, and of course, it's still amazing, even though it's tinged with sweat from his run. "Hey," he whispers, tipping my chin up and forcing me to meet his gaze. His finger is calloused, but his eyes are soft, the rings of deep forest green shining in the morning sun. "I loved every moment of it. Seeing you come undone, listening to the sounds you make when you're about to come, watching the way you writhe with my mouth on your pussy. It was heaven."

Oh my God. "Reid!" I hiss, burying my face in my hands again.

He laughs louder. "I absolutely adore flustering you, Willa Dean Dash." He leans down to peck me on the cheek. "Now, let's get me Midnight so you can go to work."

Goldie knows something is up the second she sees me from her perch at the counter rolling silverware. "Willa Dean Dash!" she hisses, waving me over. "Did you…oh my gosh! You and Reid—"

I clap a hand over her mouth and shush her. "Dad is literally feet away, and I don't know where Mom is—"

"Bathroom," she mumbles behind my hand.

"And I don't need either of them to know my business," I finish, removing my hand and wiping it on my jeans.

Goldie grins. "But did you? Because you're all…glowy."

I swear my cheeks are going to be permanently red for as much as I'm blushing. "He, um…"

"Willa, get back here," Dad calls.

Goldie's eyes are bright with merriment as she shoos me into the kitchen.

Swinging through the door, I grab an apron and tie it around my waist, then wash my hands. I drop into the comforting pattern of prepping for the morning's brunch crowd, cracking eggs and slicing tomatoes, potatoes, peppers, and onions, and, of course, wiping away the stray tears that accompany the diced onions. I pull the first ten loaves of bread from the back, lining them against the wall for easy access, and listen to Dad complain about his knees.

"You need a vacation, Dad." It's the response I always give him when he starts to complain. I know better than to tell him to retire because that's a no-go. He and Mom are still young, only in their sixties, and not yet ready to be finished with the diner. And I'm not ready for them to be finished, either. I love working beside them and my sister. Maybe most people would break out in hives at the idea of working so closely with their family, but I love it. I love getting to hear about the rest of their days outside the diner and listen to their quiet bickering over this and that. And other than Matty, Goldie is my best friend. I can't imagine not having her in my daily orbit. There's so much to love about them and this town.

Dad chooses this exact moment to ask how my night went, and Goldie pipes up, "Yeah, Willa, how'd last night go?"

I shoot her a death glare through the window. "Good. Had a nice day off."

"Reid came over," Goldie coos meaningfully.

"He did?" Mom reappears, her voice full of excitement.

Dad harrumphs.

I blush.

"He's such a nice young man," Mom says.

"Talented, too," Goldie piles on.

I'm going to kill her later.

"So what did you do?" Mom pops her head into the window as I prep the lemons.

"Just hung out." I pray I sound innocent.

Mom beams while Goldie waggles her eyebrows behind her back. "That's wonderful, honey."

"Yep," Goldie adds. *Wonderful.*

Matty appears midway through the shift, and I swing out of the kitchen to say hello.

"Goldie tells me Reid came over yesterday." His eyes glitter mischievously. "You have a good time?"

I groan. I'm never going to hear the end of it from them. "Could you be a little quieter?" I ask, keeping my voice low as I pour him a cup of coffee and gesture at the two old men at the opposite end of the counter. "Tom and Jerry are right there."

"We already know about your date with Officer Reid," Jerry calls.

I nearly drop the coffee pot. Who knew the old geezer had such good hearing? "Oh," I say weakly.

Goldie swings over and mercifully lowers her voice. "Quick, tell us what happened."

I sigh. "He, um..."

Matty chuckles, and Goldie offers, "Went down on you?"

"Oh my God," I mutter, again beyond embarrassed. "Not in front of Matty."

Matty pats my hand. "Willa, you've seen me shoulder-deep in a cow, helping it give birth. Not like I'm unfamiliar with how this works."

"Are you comparing a calf birth to hooking up, Matty?" Goldie says in mock outrage.

"Oh my God, will you two shut up," I hiss as Jerry leans closer. I glare at him, and he leans back toward Tom. Lowering my voice, I relent. "Fine. He came over, we hung out all day, it was awesome. Then he, um—"

"Ate you out," Goldie supplies.

My entire body is on fire. I clear my throat. "And then I fell asleep."

Goldie's eyes bug out. "You...fell *asleep*?"

Matty guffaws.

"I hate you both," I mumble, spinning away.

"No, no, no, wait," Goldie wheezes, grabbing my arm to keep me in place. "I need to understand how in the world this could have—"

"Willa!" Dad calls. "Break's over."

Saved by Dad. Before I can overthink it, I lean over the counter and lower my voice. I want to get this over with, and since it was my own mouth that got me into this mess, I need to get out of it. "It was the best orgasm of my life, he told me to relax, and the next thing I know I'm waking up at two in the morning. I swear it's like the man drugged me."

"He just orgasmed you," Goldie proclaims. "Congratulations."

"Maybe stay awake next time," Matty offers helpfully. "Never know what could happen next."

"We are never talking about this again." *Because what happened last night will never happen again.* Cheeks burning, I turn around to head back to cook.

The next time I turn to the window, Matty studies me. "What?"

He smiles and shrugs. "I know you want to stay in Lucky. But maybe this is an opportunity you should really consider."

I flatten my lips and shake my head. "Not happening." I make sure to say that nice and loud. Then I turn away.

Goldie had insinuated the same thing earlier, as well. Everyone is so insistent on me leaving town, but no one understands that I love it here. And following a man to Miami? A cop, no less? Reid is amazing, without question, but no. I'll never leave Lucky. Whatever last night was with Reid, it needs to end. No matter how, ahem, *talented* the man obviously is, and no matter how improbable it is that Reid was even interested in someone like me in the first place. A big-city cop and a small-town diner cook will never work, so why bother trying?

CHAPTER 14

REID

IF YOU'D TOLD me a month ago that I'd be living in a tiny beach town in Alabama, pining over a diner cook, I would have said you were crazy. And yet, here we are.

The worst part? Willa is avoiding me.

We had what I would have definitely defined as a "moment," and the woman is avoiding me. I'm over here straight-up yearning like an angsty teenager, trying to get her attention whenever I go to the diner. And sure, she looks up and smiles at me, and we're still trading Midnight duty, but she has put me on ice.

Now is probably when I should remind myself that I was only at her house a day and a half ago. But still.

I send a silent apology to the handful of women I've sent packing in the past.

Fine: ghosted. I've ghosted a few. Is this my punishment? If so, consider the message received. I'm tempted to find those women on social media and apologize, because if this is how I am after being treated as though I *didn't* have my head between her legs, then shit. I know it wasn't that the experience was bad for her. That much was obvious. But hell if I can figure out what's going on.

This morning was no different from the others: Willa showed up, handed over Midnight, and absolutely refused to make eye contact or say more than a few words to me. I'm so out of my element that all I can do is cuddle the kitten and wish she were Willa. Midnight, on the other hand, purrs like a maniac the second she gets into my hands. I'm trying to let that be my comfort, but a purring Midnight is a far cry from a Willa writhing in ecstasy.

After my requisite inspection of the property and review of the night's video—nothing out of the ordinary—I bundle up the black ball of floof, and we head to the station. Chief gives a quick rundown of the day's brief, then Ox and I head out.

It's a beautiful late summer day, and we walk toward the beach. It's a small little thing, nothing like the miles of shore we have in Miami, but it's beautiful, with deep swells of powdery-white sand leading to the teal-blue warmth of the Gulf. We don't go onto the beach itself, but stroll along the area just before it. The place is, of course, crawling with people. A few older couples here and there, but mostly this is all for families with young kids. Little toddlers, sticky with popsicles and summer sweat, and their parents, loaded down with far more beach gear than they ever thought possible. But underneath the harried expressions, it's easy to see smiles of love and appreciation. For the most part, anyway. There are definitely some folks who are downright irritated.

"Ah, family vacations," Ox intones, reading my mind as we step to the side for one such family, the dad loaded down with bags and the mom with a baby on one hip, a toddler on another, and yelling at two more to slow down as they race toward the beach.

I huff a laugh. "A far different beach scene than Miami."

"I believe it," Ox says. "You miss it?"

"Miami? I don't know. I grew up there. Well, Fort Lauderdale. It's kind of all I've ever known."

Ox whistles. "I can't imagine anything but small beach town life. But I was raised here, and love it."

I do the calculations in my head. "You went to school with Willa?"

Ox shifts a knowing glance my way. "I did."

He doesn't offer anything else. On a sigh, I push for more. "And?"

"And what, Officer MacKinnon?" he asks shrewdly.

"Come on, man."

He grins. "She's good people, Reid. She always was, and she always will be. And she makes a killer cheeseburger."

I laugh and drop it. I tried getting any amount of information out of Agatha yesterday, as well. While she seemed amenable to my pain, she was also quick to tell me that if I were really inter-ested in Willa, I'd have to figure out a way to convince her to leave town with me.

Well. I may not know Willa as well as others around here, but after our conversations, I know she's not leaving Lucky. Not even close.

What I'm beginning to realize, though, is that maybe I want to stay in Lucky, too.

Which, honestly, is ridiculous. Why would I trade Miami for, well, *this*? I like the hustle of Miami. The lights, the glitz, even the seedy parts. Hell, it's my job to like the seedy parts, and there's not really much of that here, unless you count the teenager who was caught shoplifting the other day.

After my shift with Ox, I take Midnight to Matty for a check-up. I carry her in, cradled against me like she's grown accustomed to, and the receptionist practically undresses me with her eyes. She's cute, too, and definitely my standard type: blond, big breasts, lots of make-up, smells good, bubbly, probably amenable to whatever I want. And even though she tries her best to flirt with me before going back to get Matty, it falls flat. All I can see is Willa, a woman who is the exact opposite of what I'd normally go for.

Willa is…she might be perfect. No one but Willa would spend the day in pajamas and no make-up with me. No one but Willa has moved beneath me like that. No one but Willa has given herself over so completely, and lost herself to the pleasure without worrying what she looked like. I'm a goner.

And that's a problem.

"Hey, Reid," Matty says, coming into the exam room and giving Midnight a perfunctory scratch beneath her chin. She flicks her tail in response. "How's she been?"

"Willa? Good, I guess?"

Matty quirks a knowing smile at me, already beginning his inspection of the fuzzball that's growing on me. "I meant the kitten, officer."

My neck heats in response. Busted. "Right. Midnight's been good. Putting weight on the leg, all that jazz."

"You're letting her walk around a lot, right?" he asks with a nod at the sling I'm wearing.

"Yeah. But I still take her on rounds with me. It's nice." Another thing I definitely could not do in Miami: just roll up to one of the Bunnies' strongholds with a kitten in tow. That would not go over well.

Matty takes off the cast, checks the leg, then wraps it in gauze and another bandage. "This one is a lot more forgiving. Her bones are healing up nicely, so this will give her a lot more range of motion. She's doing great. You and Willa make a good team."

I say nothing. I've already said too much.

"You like her, don't you?" Matty asks, studying me.

I stiffen. "Midnight's a great little partner."

Matty scoffs. "Come on, Reid. I'm her best friend. You think I don't know what's going on?"

"Nothing's going on." *Not that I wouldn't like it to be.*

"She's special, Reid." Matty's voice is tight, holding a warning in it. His worry for her is touching, but it's also a little insulting.

I pin him with my best glare, but Matty is wholly unaffected. "I know she is. Believe me."

Matty finishes with his inspection of Midnight and gives her a final scratch. "She's not seen a lot of the world, Reid. And in some ways, that's beautiful. But she's skittish. Never really understood why. She's got a lot to offer someone."

My throat tightens. I hear everything he's saying, and more importantly, I hear everything he isn't. "I know," I repeat. "I'm well aware of everything she has to offer, Matty."

"God knows I've tried to get her to leave this town. She could be so much bigger than she is here. But she doesn't want to leave." He stares at me, making sure I understand what he's saying.

I hold his gaze, exhaling softly. "Yeah, I know." They're the only damn words that I can manage to get out right now.

He nods. "Okay. I love her, man."

My blood heats at his words, confusion and a ridiculous sense of irrational jealousy flooding my veins. "Wait a minute. You two—"

"No way," he says, again looking at me and seeing far more than I'd prefer. "It's never been like that. Never will be. She really is my best friend. No more, no less."

The way my shoulders sag in relief should be concerning, not going to lie. Instead, I attempt some deep breaths to calm down.

"But if you break her heart..." He makes a slashing motion across this throat with his finger.

I laugh. "I'm standing here with a loaded gun in my holster, and *you're* threatening *me*?"

He shrugs. "I said what I said."

Midnight meows on the table between us, and I'm pretty sure she agrees with Matty.

On the way home, with Midnight curled up in the sling on the passenger seat of my truck, Dad calls.

"Hey," I answer through my truck speakers.

"Long time," Dad says.

"Been busy," I give him. "But you're right. I should have called."

"Busy? How is Lucky, Alabama, busy? I know from visiting there with your mom that it's as sleepy of a beach town as it can get, minus the tourists, I guess."

"Yeah…" I start.

"Oh, shit." It's a declaration.

Here's the thing. My old man has always been able to read me like a damn book, whether in person or over the phone. Judging by his immediate response to my one-word reply, he's figured me out. "Go on," I sigh. "Say it."

"You're hung up on someone, aren't you?"

I turn on my blinker and head east. "A woman."

Dad hoots. "Big-city man falling for a small-town girl? I think I've seen that movie."

"Shut up."

"Not on your life," he chuckles. "Wait till I tell your mother— hell, wait till I tell Samantha. Between the two of them, they'll have wedding invitation designs waiting in your inbox by next week."

"I'm not that bad," I protest weakly. But I probably am that bad. Last time I brought a girl home was high-school prom, so this is breaking news as far as Mom and my stepmother are concerned. And Dad will absolutely, 100 percent, be hanging up with me and telling them immediately.

"Come on." His voice is warm. "Tell me all about her."

Even knowing that he'll blab everything, I don't hesitate. I need someone to lay it all out to, and he's always been my sounding board. "Her name is Willa. She's incredible, Dad. Like no one else I've ever met."

"Apparently so. Your voice sounds like you've got stars in your eyes."

I chuckle. "She's a cook at her family's diner, but her cooking—she might give Samantha a run for her money."

Dad sucks in a breath. "Son, watch your tone. My wife is the best cook, period." His teasing is like a warm bath, and it makes my chest ache. I miss shooting the shit with him in the backyard.

"I don't know why she's got me so tied in knots. I barely know her."

Dad's observant laugh is the balm I didn't know I needed. "Sounds like you know enough. What's her favorite drink?"

"Ice-cold Cherry Coke after her shifts at the diner," I supply, the answer coming immediately. "I also know she has a standing pedicure appointment every two weeks, and that she always gets them done siren red."

I hear Dad's signature snap. If we were in person, he'd be pointing at me. "Then I think you know the answer, son."

But that can't be right. How in the hell have I been bewitched by a shy, small-town diner cook?

CHAPTER 15

WILLA

LIKE EVERY SUNDAY that I have off, it's yoga-and-a-pier-stroll with Matty. And if anyone needs to bend and stretch and push themselves to empty their brain of a certain hot policeman next door, it's me. I've tried ignoring him the best as I can. What happened the other night can't happen again.

I mean, let's be clear: I want it to happen again. Repeatedly. Daily. I could live in that experience and be perfectly content. But he's scary. He's too much: too confident, too dangerous, too gorgeous, too police-y. He's everything I never wanted. And yes, this is precisely where I'm supposed to list out the kind of person I *do* want, but every time I try to recall my list, it poofs away and reveals Hottie McHotFace himself instead of what I actually want.

Every time I see him, it's clear he wants more. More of *what*, I couldn't say. But my control is flailing. I've given the wand in my bedside table far more workouts these days than ever before, and it's all because of Reid and his chest and his tongue and his legs and…well. Everything.

But for the next ninety minutes, I'm going to get some peace.

I've got my back to the door when a buzz seems to move

through the air. I turn, and my limbs stiffen, then liquefy. Because the very man who won't leave my brain or my fantasies is now strolling into the yoga studio with a kitten strapped to his chest, looking sinfully, irrevocably hot.

Fighting the urge to fan my face, I rip my eyes away from him, say a prayer for my frayed nerves, and snap my yoga mat in the air, glaring at Matty as I bend to arrange it on the shiny wooden floor in front of me. "Really?" I hiss, fully aware of how literally everyone in the studio, woman and man, have turned to look at the deliciousness that is Reid with pussy.

Reid with a kitten, I mean.

A kitten. A fuzzy, four-legged creature.

Jesus Christ.

Matty, who is wholly unaffected by the performance that Reid is giving solely by existing, shrugs and grins at me. "Give him a chance, Willa."

I sigh. That's impossible, and Matty knows it. In mere moments, Midnight has been loosed and is running to pounce on my feet, her fuzzy black hair sticking straight up all over her tiny body as though she's just been struck by lightning, and Reid is strolling toward me in black athletic shorts and a loose tank. My stomach flip-flops.

Dear lord, I whisper, *help me to be strong.*

"Good morning," Reid says as he comes up and unrolls his mat beside me.

I force a smile and command my body to get a hold of itself.

His grin is blinding. "Matty said you'd be here and invited me. I've never done yoga. Is it hard?"

Your muscles are hard is what my brain helpfully supplies in response. And while I manage to bite that back, I *don't* manage to keep my eyes to myself. There's no stopping the way they roam over his broad chest and muscular arms and long fingers. Fingers that have been inside me, stroking me to heights I have never reached before.

Focus. I need to focus. I take control of myself again and meet his eyes, which are freaking *twinkling*. "It's...challenging. This class isn't meant for beginners."

He shrugs, moving those rock-hard shoulders up and down. "Guess I'll do my best."

Thirty minutes later, it's all I can do to maintain any kind of concentration, let alone sanity, as Midnight wends around the room and Reid stretches, bends, and *breathes* next to me. Never in my life did I think that yoga was erotic.

Now?

Now, I think that Reid could make a mint selling videos of him doing yoga and breathing. Holy. Mother. Of God. I need help.

Matty smirks next to me.

"I hate you," I mouth.

He widens his eyes and purses his mouth, his version of *"Shut up and let the man give you more orgasms."*

But I can't. Because he's going to leave. And what's the point of getting all up in my feels with the man if he's going to bolt?

Never mind the orgasm. Maybe me passing out afterward was my body's way of protecting myself.

Because mouthwatering Reid just caught me watching him.

He winks, dipping into a pose like he's most definitely done this before.

My heart hitches as I look away. God*dammit*.

After yoga, Matty very unhelpfully invites Reid to go with us to the pier.

Reid beams. "I'd love to. You wouldn't mind, right, Willa?"

"Um, no?"

"Great! It's nice to finally get some quality time with you." He raises his eyebrows and smirks.

I huff. It's clear that he and Matty have hoodwinked me into this entire operation, and I don't like it. I glare at Matty, who makes a show of ignoring me.

Reid plucks Midnight off the floor, and she takes up her

rightful residence in the sling against his chest. I'm not gonna lie, I'm beginning to have a rather unhealthy jealousy of that damn kitten.

Who I love.

Who is incredibly lucky and has no idea how many women, me especially, would kill to be snuggled up against Reid MacKinnon's chest.

Sigh.

We've barely begun our walk to the end of the pier before a shout comes from behind us. "Wait up!"

I turn and smile, grateful for the backup. "Hey, sis!"

Goldie wraps me in a hug, breathless from her sprint to join us. "You didn't tell me the Willa and Matty Yoga and Pier Walk was open to others." She shoots a playful look at Reid. "Not really fair that some new-to-town stranger gets to do it when I've been asking for years."

Reid quirks a wily smile. "Did I intrude on something?"

"Yes," I say.

"Not at all." Matty's voice overrides mine as he shoves me just enough to send me stumbling into Reid's very muscular arm. I glare at my former best friend and mouth, *"Asshole."*

He smiles a shit-eating grin right back, entirely unapologetic for his meddling activities, then holds his arm out for Goldie. She threads her arm through his without hesitation, and it almost looks as though there's a faint blush on her cheeks as she does it.

Matty lets out a satisfied grunt. "Ah, look at us, spending *quality time* together."

"It's really nice," Reid agrees.

Goldie shoots a look at me, and I guess whatever she sees has her elbowing Matty in my defense.

They don't get it. I know they want to see me happy, and I love them for it. But what's the point in any of this if the only thing that waits for me at the end is Reid going back to Miami?

"Come on," I grumble. "Let's at least go check on my yacht."

Reid's head whips to me. "You have a yacht?"

We all laugh. "Hardly. But we've all claimed a vessel," I gesture to the line of beautifully appointed yachts and boats. "Mine is way down there, at the end."

Reid looks where I'm pointing. "The *Shakespeare*?"

I shake my head. "No, the really big one on the other side. The *Bear*."

He chuckles. "For someone as unassuming as you, you really swing for the fences with your boats, huh?"

I shrug. "It's a fantasy. Why not?"

We continue talking as we walk, the four of us joking and having a good time. I let myself relax into the camaraderie, and by the time we make our way back up the pier, Matty and Willa are making excuses to leave. Because of course they are.

Reid waves as they hustle away. "Are they a thing?"

I snort a laugh. "Matty and my sister? No way."

He hums thoughtfully.

I reach up to pet Midnight, and she bats at my hand playfully.

"Ride home with me?" Reid asks.

I glance up at him. "Well, considering that Matty's abandoned me, sure. I'd love to."

At the house, Reid puts his truck in park and looks over at me, where I've got Midnight bundled into a ball on my lap and purring contentedly. "Want to explain to me why you've been ignoring me?"

I freeze. "I—"

"Because I like you, Willa. I want to spend time with you. I thought you wanted the same thing. If I'm wrong—"

"You're not wrong." I regret the words as soon as they leave my mouth.

"Then what is it?"

"None of this is *real!*" I blurt, my heart racing. "You, me...it's not real." I exhale and keep my eyes on my shaking hands.

Silently, he reaches over and wraps his palms around them.

His touch is so calm, so reassuring. Finally, he speaks. "Does it feel real?"

I swallow.

"Because if it does, then maybe we take it for what it is."

"What is it?" I whisper.

"A gift," he answers softly. "A beautiful gift that I can't turn away from, no matter how hard I try."

My gaze snaps to his. Those gorgeous greens are filled with sincerity and tenderness, and his voice is thick when he speaks again. "Come over."

Yes. No. *Yes.* Never in my life have I identified more with the concept of an angel on one side and a devil on the other, arguing with each other about what their person should do.

He must see my hesitation, because his eyes darken as they sweep over my body. I feel every inch of his perusal. "Come on, Willa Dean. What's a few minutes?"

I fake a scowl. "It's just Willa."

He laughs gently and gets out of the cab, meeting me on the other side as I'm stepping out with Midnight.

"Want me to take her?"

"I've got her." I slide out of the truck, knowing that I have a choice to make: Go to my house and put the final nail in the coffin of whatever this is with Reid before it starts, or go to his and let myself enjoy him the rest of the time he's here.

CHAPTER 16

WILLA

TAKE A deep breath, then head up the stone path to his porch. Reid unlocks the door and steps back for me to enter first.

I cross the threshold, looking around as I do. It's a little too beach chic for my taste, but tidy. White walls decorated with generic prints and frames that the owner probably got from TJ Maxx, and there's an Oriental rug that's seen better days on the floor. I let Midnight down, and she immediately turns to swat at my hands, ready to do battle. We play for a minute.

When I stand and turn back around, Reid's there in front of me, his forest-green eyes deep with desire as he takes me in.

Oh, God.

I breathe in, and it's my undoing. He smells so freaking good. How can anyone smell so good after yoga and a walk on the pier?

"Willa." He exhales my name in a whisper, as though he's begging for something.

"Reid." My own voice is unsteady. I can't think when he's this close.

He reaches up and brushes my hair back, then moves my

bangs away from my eyes. I'm not sure I'm breathing. His thumb, rough and calloused and panty-melting, swipes at my cheek. Then, across my lips.

On instinct, my tongue darts out to lick it. His eyes darken even further, a predatory glint shining out of them.

"Willa." He growls it this time.

And something inside me just…snaps.

I jump into his arms, because suddenly I'm someone who does that sort of thing, and he grabs me without hesitation.

Our lips meet. This kiss isn't soft and tender. It isn't romantic. It's hot.

Teeth clash and tongues war and moans come out of the both of us as I grind my hips against him.

"Fuck, Willa." His hands dig into my rear. "Please."

"Yes." It's all I need to say before he spins and walks us to his room.

I don't stop writhing against him. I need more. More.

"You can have whatever you want," Reid answers.

A hot flush runs up my chest to my face. "Did I say that out loud?" I murmur, burying my face in his neck.

He stops in front of the bed. "You did, and it was perfect." He grins at me, everything about him pure sex, then he tosses me —*tosses* me!—onto the bed.

I land with a bounce, my heart leaping into my throat.

"Get undressed."

"Reid, I—" Then I lose my words, because the man rips his shirt off in that hot-as-sin way that men do, reaching behind his neck to pull it over his head, his stomach muscles bunching deliciously as he moves. "Fuck," I breathe.

He stands before me in running shorts and nothing else. The grin he gives me is nothing short of feral. "Take your fill, Willa. This is all yours."

I might pass out. "Water," I croak.

He barks out a laugh. "I'll go get you some water. You're going to need it." He spins to leave the room, but stops and wheels back to me. "Be naked when I get back. That's an order."

My brain short-circuits, but I manage to do exactly what he says, peeling off my shorts and sports bra and tank far quicker than I thought I had in me. Also: Let the record show that there is nothing more awkward than trying to figure out what to do with yourself when you're totally naked on a man's bed before the two of you have done anything and you're waiting on him to get back from the kitchen with water that you, for some ridiculous reason, said you needed.

I yank my hair out of its ponytail and consider: Do I lie on my side like Jeff Goldblum, all sprawled and confident and smirking? No. I'm neither confident nor prepared to sprawl. Sitting cross-legged seems weird. Maybe I do some kind of legs to the side and leaning on one arm thing? Crap. I'm still moving around the bed awkwardly, and definitely giving thanks that I took a shower this morning before yoga, when Reid walks back in.

"Good girl," he purrs, his eyes taking me in as he hands me the water. I take a sip, then he says, "You take orders so well."

I promise you, the water dribbles out of my mouth as I stare at him.

He laughs. "God, I love flustering you."

I blush furiously and wipe my mouth. "That's not fair," I whine, waving my hand at him. "You look like...*this*...and then you say things like *good girl* and talk about me obeying? What do you expect a girl to do?"

He shucks his shorts.

"Jesus fucking Christ," I whisper.

He chuckles again, his dick bobbing up and down as he does.

Listen. I've never been one to describe a dick as pretty. That's not really my thing. But Reid MacKinnon is sporting the prettiest dick I have ever seen in my life. Have I seen a lot of them? No, but that's utterly beside the point. The man clearly has invested in a trimmer, because he's also got some nice manscaping going on, but again: he has the most perfect dick, like, ever.

I don't have words.

I'm babbling in my dang head, for goodness' sake.

"What you don't seem to understand, Willa," Reid says, putting one knee on the bed, "is that *you* are the one who's not fair. *You* are the one who renders me utterly speechless. *You*, with your pajamas and shorts and tank tops." He begins to crawl up the bed, a lion stalking its prey, his eyes dark and feral as he takes me in. "I have imagined this for weeks."

I squeak, utterly paralyzed in the face of him.

He grins, a fantasy so good I never dared imagine it come to life. When he speaks, his voice is low and dark. "Spread your legs for me, pretty girl."

I obey. My arms shake, threatening to give way as Reid crawls between my legs, hovering over me.

"Breathe," he commands.

I gulp in a breath, lightheaded. I apparently hadn't been breathing. "See?" I croak. "I can't function around you."

He shakes his head. "It's a goddamn wonder I can even *think* around you, Willa Dean Dash. Now," he says, his hand cupping my chin and forcing me to meet his eyes, "you're going to let me worship you like the goddess you are. You're going to let me make you come, over and over and over. Right?"

I nod dumbly.

"Give me your words, Willa."

"Y-yes," I stammer.

"What's your safe word?"

"M-my safe word?" I squeak.

He nods. "I'm not holding back with you, sweetheart. But I don't want to hurt you or scare you. What's your safe word?"

"Avocado." It's the first word that comes to mind.

He barks a laugh, breaking the tension, but still holding himself over me. I smile, then start to giggle.

"Avocado?" he says, his voice filled with amused warmth.

"It's the first thing you gave me trouble over."

He licks his lips. "That I did." He's still gripping my chin, but now he loosens his hold and scrapes his thumb over my lower lip again.

I bite it.

His eyes flare. "You wanna play, Willa?"

I have no idea what's about to happen, but if it's happening with him? Absolutely. I want All The Things. Whatever they are. "Yes."

He growls. "Good answer." Then he jerks his head to his bedside table. "Condoms are in there. Trust that I'll have one on when I decide you're worthy of having my cock."

Oh my God. A whimper escapes me, and my whole body explodes in a riot of goosebumps. "Okay," I whisper.

Reid gives me a filthy grin in response, then descends, letting his weight settle on me, and I make a sound of pleasure.

His answering groan and thrust of his hips is enough to make me lift my knees eagerly. He laughs darkly. "Put your legs down, Willa."

I do as he says, and he claims my mouth in a searing kiss, the scruff of his light beard abrading against my skin as his tongue delves past mine, his hand skimming down my body to grab my rear and squeeze. I whimper into his mouth, scrabbling for purchase on his back.

When he pulls his lips from mine, it's to trail hot, wet kisses down my neck to my breast, where he immediately latches on to suck.

My back bows in response, heat pooling between my legs. I'm already out of my mind with want and need.

"So fucking responsive," he says, his eyes meeting mine. "These tits, Willa. Perfect. Absolutely perfect." Then he takes my nipple into his mouth again, swirling and sucking while his other hand mimics the movement of his tongue on my other breast.

I thread my hand through his too-short hair, writhing at the sensation. "Too much," I manage to gasp.

He eases up, but doesn't stop. I wiggle more, the sensations almost too much to bear, my teeth grinding as spikes of pleasure radiate through me.

Without a word, he pulls off me and kneels, grabs my leg, and flips me over. My cheek presses into the mattress as he flattens his body over mine, his dick hard against my ass. He breathes against the back of my ear, sending shivers down my body. Then he kisses my neck and continues his trail, kissing my shoulders, nipping at my skin, his hands seemingly everywhere at once. It's a riot of sensations, and all I can do is breathe.

"You're doing so well, Willa," Reid says behind me. "You ready for your first reward?"

I press my hips into the mattress, desperate for relief. Without warning, his palm smacks my butt. "What was that?" I squeal.

"I didn't say you could move, Willa." His voice is a little dark and a lot sexy.

Oh.

I stop wiggling, but there's no stopping the whimper that escapes. "I need…"

He straddles me, the warmth of his thighs around my hips somehow insanely erotic as he moves my hair off my face. "You obey me so well, Willa." He gathers my hair into his hand and pulls just a little, sending a thrill of excitement through me.

"Do you like that?" he murmurs against my ear.

I nod, afraid of what I'll say if I speak.

"You want it harder?"

I want *everything*. "Yes."

He tightens his grip, exposing the side of my throat to his mouth for him to suck and bite. I start to wiggle again, but he yanks on my hair. "No moving," he admonishes. "You're about to get your reward, remember?"

Vaguely, I recall something about that, but all I know is I want to do whatever he tells me to.

He gives my hair one final tug before letting it go and sliding back down my body. His lips trace a path down my back to one of my butt cheeks, then he bites it. "This ass, my God. It has featured prominently in my fantasies."

I suck in a breath.

He chuckles, then bites it again. "Yes, Willa. I've absolutely gotten myself off to thoughts of you. Do you like knowing that?"

"Yes," I breathe, fighting so hard to keep still. "Please," I whisper.

He growls. "Please, what?"

"Please let me move." I'm desperate for relief. "I need —"

He sits up. "Raise your hips, pretty girl. Let me see you."

"W-what?" I stammer, unsure.

He repeats himself. "Raise your hips, Willa, and show me your pretty pussy. I'd like to eat it."

Oh. My. God.

He smacks my ass. "Now."

Immediately, I raise my hips, my brain exploding from his words.

"On your knees. Chest on the mattress."

I adjust myself as directed.

"There we go," he praises. "Look at you. Glistening. Waiting for me."

I whimper. "Can I move?"

He pops my ass again. "No."

"Fuck." My heart is racing, and the word is breathy when it comes out. I grip the comforter, needing something solid to remind me that this is real. That this intense feeling of euphoria and naughtiness and eroticism is all happening, and it's *real*. And

I want more. So much more. Something inside me unfurls and turns toward the light that is Reid.

"This is your first time, isn't it?" he asks softly. "Being controlled like this."

I nod, trying to breathe normally.

He trails a finger up the back of my calf and thigh, then over my butt and down the other thigh and calf. He continues the pattern, getting closer and closer to where I need him, but never close enough. "Reid, please," I beg.

He brings his mouth to my ass, kissing and biting it. "You ready for me to put my mouth on your gorgeous pussy, Willa?"

This man and his naughty mouth are going to be the death of me. "Yes," I say. I don't even sound like myself anymore. My voice is guttural, animalistic. "Please."

He hums behind me. "I like the way you say please, Willa. I'm grabbing my cock right now, and I want to shove it into you so badly, to bottom out inside you and make you scream. And I will. But not yet." He breaks off with another curse, and before I can respond, his hands are lifting my ass just enough, and his mouth is between my legs.

I jerk at the sensation of the hot, wet heat of his tongue, then groan in relief. I begin to chant. "Fuck, Reid, thank you, thank you, thank you."

It must be exactly what he needs to hear, because his mouth is performing magic. I moan, unable to contain myself and having no reason to do so, rocking my hips back and forth. Then he stops, pulling away and smacking my ass again.

"Nooo," I whine.

"Don't. Move," he snarls.

I go still, but my mouth has other ideas. "Reid, *please*," I beg.

"No." He descends again, his tongue pushing inside me.

I fight to keep still, but it's almost impossible. I fist the sheets beneath me, the only movement I'm able to do, and am nearly blinded by pleasure. "More," I manage.

He pulls away. "Turn over."

I lower myself to the bed and do as he commands, then take him in. His eyes are wild, his lips wet with me, and he's got his hand wrapped around his dick, stroking it leisurely. I take in a breath and let it out slowly, another wave of goosebumps taking over my body. "You're so sexy," I breathe, moving my hand to my pussy.

He narrows his eyes. "Absolutely not. You only touch yourself if I give you permission."

I pull my fingers away and whine, circling my hips. "Reid, I need to..."

He gives me a wicked grin. "You need to what, Willa?"

I blush furiously.

His grin softens and gets sweet. "You can say the word, Willa."

I lick my lips. "I need to come. Please let me come, Reid."

He swears, and his eyes darken even further. Then he takes a finger and runs it up between my legs, making me hiss. "Like this?"

I swallow. "Any way is good."

He gives himself a final pump, then leverages his body over mine. "Eyes on me, Willa."

My face burns. "I don't think..."

"You will watch me make you come, or you don't come at all."

I snap my eyes to him, my need overwhelming any lingering embarrassment.

With our gazes locked, Reid bends to take a lazy lick of me, running his tongue between my lips to my clit and circling.

My eyes roll back in my head.

"Eyes, Willa," Reid demands. "Give me those eyes."

I snap them open again, and he works me over, focusing exactly where I need him. Heat begins to swirl inside me, and my hips buck. When his eyes narrow, I whimper but obey, stilling my hips. He sucks my clit, and I gasp.

"Reid!" I yell.

"There you go." He sucks again while pushing a finger into me. He follows with a second finger, and it's all I need.

"Fuck, Reid, oh—" I moan, then tip over the edge, the intensity of the orgasm blinding me even as I manage to keep my eyes on his.

He works me through pulse after pulse of sweet relief, then eases up as I come down, pulling his fingers out and kissing a path up my body. He takes my mouth in a deep kiss, and I taste myself on him. I go limp when he pulls away, and something incoherent leaves my mouth, and he chuckles, sliding up to lie on his side next to me and running his fingers up and down my body.

"You are so sexy," he murmurs. "I could watch you come all day long."

I turn on my side to look at him as his dark eyes flare. "More," I say simply. "I am nowhere near done." After a moment's hesitation, I murmur, "Please."

He grins wickedly. "You think you've earned it?"

I run my hand over his chest, reveling in its hardness, the way his tan skin contrasts with the paleness of mine. There's no more bandage on his shoulder, just a neat pink circle of the healing scar. I trace my hand down to his dick and wrap my hand around it, delighting in the velvet over steel. He jerks with the contact, and I smile up at him. "Can I?"

His eyes darken. "You can do whatever you want, Willa."

I bend to him, taking his dick into my mouth immediately. I'm probably a little too enthusiastic, if I'm being honest, and I wouldn't doubt he's had better head, but I don't care. I've wanted this man's dick in my mouth, and now it's here. I taste his precum, then adjust my position, kneeling between his legs to lick and suck, enjoying the moans coming out of him.

"Fuck, just like that, Willa," he growls. "You like my cock, don't you?"

I release him with a pop. "I do." I meet his eyes. And immediately, it's crystal clear why he wanted me to look at him when the positions were reversed. The way he's looking at me, as if his very world hinges on what I do next, is powerful. To have Reid's attention on me, to know he's waiting to see what I do next, that I have his desire at my disposal and can make him writhe with it, is a heady feeling. One I could definitely get used to.

I bend to him once again, tracing the thick vein running root to tip with my tongue before taking him to the back of my throat again. He whispers encouragingly to me. "That's so good, Willa. Yes. Good girl, fuck, you like that, so do I."

I feel his legs stiffen and think I'm going to get to bring him to orgasm the same as he did for me, but he leans down to pull me off.

I pout. "But you were so close."

He grins. "Exactly."

"Don't you want to come?"

"Look at how easily you said the word," he praises.

Naturally, I flush. He rolls over to the bedside table and pulls out a condom, and I watch as he puts it on. "I like to be edged, Willa."

I blink, realization dawning. "Oh."

"So I like the wait. The build-up. That way, when I do let myself orgasm, it's more intense." He rolls me onto my back and settles between my legs. "Have you ever been edged, sweetheart?"

I shake my head. "Can we not do that today?"

He leans to take my mouth in a kiss. "I'm in charge, sweetheart." Then he pushes a finger into me. I gasp. "You ready for me?"

"Please," I manage.

He withdraws his finger and positions his dick at my entrance. "Say it again."

Something occurs to me. "Please, Officer."

His features darken and he growls as he gives me a little bit of him.

I wiggle, trying to get more. "Please, Officer MacKinnon," I say breathlessly. "Give me your dick."

"Cock."

"Cock," I repeat without hesitation. I don't recognize the person I am right now. "Please give me your cock. I need it."

"God, yes. So good." He pushes all the way in.

The pleasure is unlike anything I've ever felt, because of course it is. He goes deeper, fills me more, than anyone before him. Maybe it's his experience, maybe it's just him, but either way, it's unreal. This is…this is…God. He pushes into me, again and again, his chest glistening with sweat above me, and all I can do is moan and writhe beneath him.

Reid's eyes sear into mine. "Tell me."

"So good," I gasp, sliding my eyes away.

He grips my chin and forces me to look at him. "Look at me and tell me how much you love my cock."

My walls tighten at his words and heat rises to my cheeks. I lower my gaze, but meet his again as he pushes into me.

He smirks. "Do you have any idea how much I love making you blush, Willa?" He pulls back and slams home, and I cry out. "Even now, when I'm balls deep in you, you still blush." He pushes again, driving so far into me I think my spleen might be bruised. If that's even a thing.

"Reid," I gasp.

"Say it," he growls. "Tell me you love my cock."

"I love your cock," I grit out.

"Good. Girl," he pants, then begins to hammer into me. "Now come."

Don't have to tell me twice. I tip into oblivion at his command, gripping him tightly with my arms and legs while my walls pulse around his dick. "Fuck!" I yell, coming so hard I think I might pass out.

Reid slams into me, over and over, until he finally makes one last thrust and holds, pulsing inside me while he yells my name.

We cling to each other, breathing hard, for what feels like minutes. Eventually, I relax, and he pulls out of me, rolling to the side and jumping up to dispose of the condom.

When he returns, he hauls me to him, giving me no choice in the matter.

"You're staying here," he gruffs, his breath tickling my neck.

I wiggle my butt against him, happy once again to obey.

CHAPTER 17

WILLA

MY FIRST THOUGHT upon waking is how sore I am, followed immediately by wondering if I'd been drugged. I slept like a rock. Easily the best sleep in years.

Is this how I sleep after having orgasms? If so, I clearly need more of them in my life.

I stretch and extend my arm, fully expecting it to land on a deliciously hard chest. One that's connected to a set of abs I'd like to lick. Instead, I find a cold mattress.

Oh.

Fighting the urge to make myself small, I pull the covers over me and sit up, looking around like I'm going to find him, even though I can tell by the sound of the house that he's gone. The sensation of knowing I'm here, alone, is gutting.

This was a mistake.

I make quick work of getting dressed, and even though I know no one is here, I still tiptoe out. The battle to stand tall and strong is lost, and I'm as tiny and insignificant as the little black kitten I find curled up on her bed in the living room, asleep.

He left Midnight. Maybe this is his way of telling me that I need to forget this ever happened. Which, fair, but I can't promise that future men won't have a heck of a high bar to meet in the bedroom.

I peek out the back door, scouting far and wide for any signs of Reid, Agatha, or anyone else. The coast is clear. I sprint across his backyard and onto the driveway that leads to my little cottage. It's only when I'm inside, my heart bruised and unsure, that I realize how much I wanted to see Reid out there waiting, fresh takeout coffee from the coffee shop in hand, smiling and popping those glorious dimples of his as he wished me good morning.

Guess not.

I inhale deeply, shake my whole body like it's going to get rid of the feel of him, and take a shower. It doesn't work. With every minute that goes by, another ghost of his touch passes over my skin. Memories of last night slam into me, one after the other, until I'm a pathetic mess.

It's absolutely slammed at work. It's too busy for me to be distracted, but distracted I am. On top of that, everyone else is just as off-kilter as me. I mess up orders and put us behind, but all he does is grunt and keep going. Even Tom and Jerry aren't here.

The whole thing feels odd.

A couple hours into opening, JJ comes in. My ears perk up when Mom asks him why he looks so disheveled.

"There was a massive wreck just outside of town," he answers, pulling the steaming cup of coffee toward him like it's going to save his life.

"Willa," Dad says. "Hash browns."

I wave him off, my attention riveted on JJ. "You flip 'em. Not like you weren't cooking by yourself for years before I got here."

He harrumphs but doesn't argue, and I refocus back on the counter.

"Too early to tell what really happened, but it's a four-car wreck. No fatalities—"

"Amen," the full counter offers.

"Amen," JJ answers. "But at least two went to the hospital. Every officer in a twenty-five-mile radius got called to the scene to help out."

So that's where Reid is. But knowing it doesn't make me feel any better; it does the opposite. I'm absolutely certain I'm being a brat about the situation, but I welcome it. Anything to protect myself.

"Willa." Dad's voice is stern. "There are knives and fifty ways to Sunday to get yourself burned back here. Either do your job or get out of my kitchen."

Ouch. But he's right. Same as Reid is apparently doing his. I turn back to the griddle, throwing a serving of hash browns on, then cracking eggs for a bird's nest over easy. I plate the browns, then grab four slices of white bread, running them over the butter mill before plopping them down on the far right of the griddle.

"Drop four waffles, two Bennies, and pull four links," comes Goldie's voice from behind me. Then, "What is this? Willa, I needed them scrambled, not...whatever this is."

I turn to grab the offending plate without missing a beat. "Gimme sixty," I say, then hustle to scramble the eggs and drop them onto the griddle. Flip the toast, pull off the hash browns, scoop the bird's nest, and plate the eggs to hand back to Goldie. "Hang on, and I'll give you table ten."

She raises an eyebrow, but stays in place. In moments, the other meals are plated, and she's off.

I grab another ticket, but I can't stop the niggling worry at the back of my head. *He's a cop.*

A very hot cop with out-of-this-world-talent, but a cop nonetheless. The job is inherently dangerous, even in a tiny town like ours.

And he's leaving. I have to remember that. Two more months, and he's gone. I can't let myself fall for this guy, King of Orgasms or not.

"Focus, Willa," I mutter, then stride to the walk-in to grab another bin of sausages. Disappearing in the middle of the night might be standard for a police officer. Is that something I'm prepared to deal with?

It doesn't matter. Two months. That's it.

The shift is seventy-billion years long. I check my phone like the loser I am, hoping for a text from Reid, but there's nothing. I pull off my apron and toss it into the bin with a sigh.

"Okay, what is with you?" Goldie asks, sidling up to me from nowhere and pinning me with those gold-flecked eyes of hers. "Something's happened, but we were too busy for me to ask."

"I—" I start, then clamp my mouth shut.

"Come on," Goldie wheedles, poking at my side to get me to smile. "This isn't like you. Tell your little sis Goldie and let her fix it."

I can't help the small laugh that escapes me. "I'm not ready to talk about it, O Great One," I say, forcing a grin to ease the sting. "Can I get back to you?"

Her face falls. "Oh. Okay. Sure."

Something tells me I should probably talk to her, but all I want to do is go home and bury myself under my blankets. After a shower.

Reid's truck is in his driveway when I get home. I can't remember if it was there this morning or not, but it doesn't matter. I make a point of staring straight ahead when I walk down the driveway and into my house. And sure, I should probably be a good kitten parent and go ask for Midnight, but I just...I can't. I don't want to know if he's in his house being all sexy and broody, or if he's sitting outside doing the same, strumming on his guitar like a long-lost country singer.

For the record, I don't much like country music, unless it's coming out of Reid MacKinnon's mouth.

The door snicks shut behind me without so much as a peep from next door. Probably for the best.

I put my phone on mute and leave it charging in the kitchen. Then I head for the shower.

CHAPTER 18

REID

THIS HAS BEEN the day from hell. The absolute worst kind. Being woken up by my uncle calling me to work a massive pile-up that shouldn't have happened, but someone was drinking and driving, and the 18-wheeler behind them couldn't react fast enough. The pile-up was chaos, but not deadly.

I left so fast that I was in the middle of working the accident before I realized I'd not so much as left a note for Willa. Considering she'd been naked and sleeping soundly in the early dawn light of my bedroom, it was the worst kind of asshole move.

Even sorrier was the tiny thrill I got as I drove to the scene. Finally, something was happening in this sleepy town.

I'm not sure which was worse: no note for Willa, or being excited at an accident. Both are terrible.

Paperwork and phone calls took up most of the rest of the day, and then my Miami chief called.

I strode into Jack's office. "What's up?"

He nodded at the phone on speaker. "Chief Muñoz, I've got Reid."

"Hey, Chief."

He launched without preamble. "Things have taken a turn. You need to lie low—real low."

My gut twisted. "What's the damage?"

"DA didn't have enough to hold our guy. Let the bastard out two days ago and just now got around to telling me."

My blood went cold, then immediately boiled. "*What?*"

"That's about what I said. We've gotten word that he's looking for you. Any cover you might have had is totally blown, and there's a hefty bounty out for you."

"Shit." I ran my hands through my hair, my thoughts running a thousand miles a minute. This was bad. Very bad.

"Just stay low, MacKinnon," Chief cautioned. Then he clicked off.

I didn't need to look at my uncle to know he was thinking the same thing: between JJ's ridiculous cover stories and relentless coverage of what he'd now dubbed "The Kitten Cop," I was the farthest thing from low.

And now it's the afternoon, and Willa has the balls to walk right by the house without so much as a glance my way.

Well, fuck that.

After making sure Midnight has her dinner, I lock my house up and stomp over to Willa's.

I knock, but there's no answer. She's probably in the shower.

I try the door, which is unlocked and incredibly stupid. It's never a good idea on a regular day to be so exposed, but now? With the danger she's in because of me? My gut twists. I enter the house, lock it, then stalk to her bedroom to wait.

I don't have long. She walks into the room dripping wet, a tiny purple towel doing little to hide her curves from my ravenous eyes.

She yelps. "Jesus, Reid! What are you doing?"

"You need to lock your door," I growl.

She opens her mouth, then closes it when my words register.

I fold my arms across my chest.

Her eyes narrow into tiny slits. "So, you bolt in the middle of the night, and now you're breaking into my house to order me around?"

"I didn't break in. It was *unlocked*."

"I didn't *let you in*," she counters. "Therefore, you broke in!"

I stand and close the distance between us, raking my eyes over her body. Droplets of water cling to the pale skin of her shoulders, and I'm aching to pull her to me. My cock twitches, but I'm apparently committed to being an asshole, because the next words out of my mouth are, "Pretty sure I'm better acquainted with the civil code than you, sweetheart."

"You've been here a month. How much could you possibly know?" she scoffs, backing against the wall as I crowd her.

She smells fucking delicious, some kind of vanilla and brown sugar combo that's driving me wild. A bead of water drips from her hair onto her collarbone, and I'm so desperate to touch her that I run my finger over her skin to catch the drop. Her breath hitches, and I lift my finger away, putting it into my mouth and sucking on it. Her eyes darken. I lower my voice. "Why don't you trust that I know all about entering things, Willa?"

She flushes, her creamy skin splotching with embarrassment at my words. "Leave."

I smirk. "You don't mean that."

She licks her lips and juts her chin up. "Then tell me, Reid, what *do* I mean?"

"Look at you, being a little brat," I murmur, moving so close that her chest touches mine with every shaky inhale she takes. "Did I pound that brattiness into you last night when I fucked you?" She gasps, and I grab her hand to flatten it against my stiff-as-hell cock. "See, my little Willa, I think what you really mean is that you want this." Then I pull her off the wall to press her against me. Immediately, she softens, so I know I'm reading her correctly. "And I think you want me to worship your luscious body in the way it was meant to be worshipped: one inch at a time."

Her eyes flash. "I don't think I like you."

I chuckle darkly and rip her towel off. "I think you do. And you know what?"

She's trembling now, but I know it's with anticipation because she's angling closer, rising on her tiptoes, her pupils blown with lust. "What?" she whispers.

"I'm just the man to do it."

With that, I pick her up, and she wraps her legs around my waist, grinding against me without hesitation.

"Fine," she mutters, leaning in for a kiss.

I let her control it. She's angry and rattled, and she pours every emotion into the kiss as she digs her short nails into my skin. And I want it. I want all of her. All her thoughts, all her fears, all her hopes and dreams. Groaning, I spin us to lay her on the bed, taking in all her beautiful curves. She's still so innocent, trusting implicitly that I'll take care of her, and every instinct in me roars to possess her, protect her, make her mine.

She's fucking perfect. Two months isn't enough.

Shoving that thought out of my head, I toe off my shoes and socks and get undressed, trying hard not to preen under her watchful gaze. Without a word, I yank her to the edge of the bed and sink to my knees, burying my face between her legs.

Her response is immediate, and I lose myself in her, relishing the yank of her hands on my hair, the way she bucks against my face, the way her legs shake and tremble as she comes. Her taste. Dear God in heaven, her *taste*.

I need more. Crave it. She clings to me as I crawl up her body and she locks her gaze on me, her eyes still glassy. "Reid," she breathes.

"Tell me you have condoms."

She points in the direction of her bedside drawer. Wordlessly,

I grab them and toss them on the mattress, then pull her to me, guiding her up to straddle me.

"Fuck, you look good like this," I murmur. Her hair is still damp and falling long and tousled down her back, her bangs fluttering into her eyes. Her breasts, a perfect handful with delicate rose-pink nipples, perk up as I run my hands over them. Then I grip her waist, groaning at the way her flesh fills my hands. "These curves, Willa."

She's focused on my chest, where her hands have been running over the muscles and down, then back up again, studiously avoiding the gunshot wound. She's quiet. "I'm nothing special."

"That's a load of shit," I say, and judging by the way she jerks, it was definitely too aggressive. I soften my voice. "You're amazing. You're strong, funny, an incredible cook—"

She scoffs. "I'm well aware of how little I know, thanks to my one semester of school."

"You were the victim of an egotistical man who felt threatened by someone as young and beautiful and creative and *good* as you." I try to control my voice. I hate it when men tear women down in an effort to build themselves up.

Her eyes widen. "Did you watch it?"

I nod. "Every episode you were in. And he was an unmitigated asshole."

She worries her lower lip. "You think so?"

I grab a condom. "I know so." Then I hand it to her. "You know what else I know?"

She turns those doe eyes on me, and my cock jumps. "What?"

"That you're a naughty girl who wants to ride me like I'm her favorite toy."

She giggles self-consciously, her cheeks reddening as she ducks her head. Her long hair covers one side of her face, falling just to the tip of her nipple.

I push her hair back and wait on her to step into herself,

understanding that the brief conversation pulled her out of whatever bit of power she'd allowed herself to take. My sweet girl.

She hesitates, then pulls the condom wrapper up to her mouth and bites a corner to rip it open. My dick throbs at the sight, and I know she can feel it on her ass. "Just like that," I praise. "What are you going to do next?"

She rises and resettles on my thighs, then grips my cock and rolls the condom on. I stay as still as possible, unsure if she's even done this part before. She's experienced, but still acts like a newborn fawn with those fucking eyes of hers, flitting to mine and back like she's afraid to sustain contact.

"Want me to do something with my hands?" I ask.

She bites her lip again, her teeth sinking into her plush bottom lip, and it takes everything in me not to push my thumb into her mouth and take control. But I want to see what she can do if she's allowed the freedom to do it.

"Put your hands above your head," she whispers.

I obey instantly, then wait for her next command.

"Keep them there."

I nod. "Yes, chef."

Her eyes flare, then she angles herself above me. "Are you sure?" she asks.

I huff out a laugh. "Am I sure that I want to be fucked by a beautiful woman who's just told me to keep my hands to myself? Absolutely."

She lowers herself onto me, inch by hot, tight inch, and I grit my teeth to keep myself in check. "Fuck, Willa," I bite out.

"Is this okay?" She looks up at me, blinking through those dark bangs.

"So okay," I say, pushing farther into her and smiling at the way her eyes roll back in her head. "Are you okay?"

"Uh-huh," she whimpers.

"Find your rhythm, sweetheart," I urge. "I'll follow."

She starts slowly, undulating her lips and moving them side to side, working to find what's best. In moments, she's got it, and she braces her hands on my chest as she grins in triumph.

"There we go," I grin, pushing into her as she bears down. "Does it feel good?"

"Un...be...liev...able," she pants, her hips swirling and bucking with each syllable. "Oh my God, Reid."

"Wanna go faster?"

"Y-yes."

I thrust up, making her almost fall onto my chest. "Then do it. Ride my cock, Willa."

"Your mouth, Reid," she gasps, her cheeks flushed.

"Ride me like a cowgirl. Like a goddess. Like—"

She slaps her hand over my mouth. "Shut up."

I bite a finger, then thrust harder into her. It's difficult to keep my hands away from her ridiculous ass, but I'm managing.

Her eyes go wide as she yanks her hand away. "Did you just *bite* me?"

I grin up at her, thoroughly enjoying myself. "I did, princess. When are you gonna let me move my hands?"

She swats at me, then grinds her pussy up and down my length. We groan in unison. "With that attitude, not anytime soon," she pants.

There she is. Gratified, I thrust into her, forcing her to slap her hands back on my chest. "Fine with me, sweetheart," I say, not out of breath but not *not* out of breath. "Fuck, you're hot."

She laughs, and it makes her clench against my cock. I groan, my eyes rolling into the back of my head. "Seriously, Willa. You're going to kill me."

"Death by sex," she muses, circling her hips like a wanton goddess. "Has a nice ring to it."

"That's it," I growl. I can't take any more. I pull my arms down and grab her waist. "Hang on, sweetheart."

"Reid!" she scolds. "I didn't say you could—ah, *fuck*."

And she leans down onto me, wrapping her arms around who

the hell knows what as I pump into her from below. "Ohmygod, Reid," she moans. "Yes, yes, please don't stop."

"Not on your life," I grit, my hands digging into her flesh as I pound relentlessly into her. I've definitely pulled a back muscle, and I definitely don't give a shit. Her walls clench around my cock. "There you go. Come for me. Come for me like the good—"

"Fuck!" she screams, her hands finally finding purchase on my shoulders as her nails dig half-moons into me.

"Fuck yes," I growl, relishing the sting of her grip. "Harder, baby. Harder."

She obeys, sobbing through her orgasm.

Blinding white light shoots across my vision as I come, my entire body clenching as absolute bliss takes over. I mutter something incomprehensible, then let myself go limp.

Willa lets herself do the same, and I relish the feel of her weight on me. She's breathing hard into the crook of my neck, and I reach to pull her hair to one side, getting it off her neck so she can cool down.

"You okay?" I ask.

She chuckles, her whole body moving with the effort. "Reid, I am more than okay." Then she leans up, tucking her chin into the palm of her hand and gazing down at me. "Are *you* okay?"

I fake a grimace. "I don't know. After the bite you gave me..."

"I didn't bite you—*you* bit *me*!" She laughs again, and when she raises her arm to swat playfully at me, I grab it, turning it so I can kiss her palm. Her gaze softens as I do it.

Then, because I can't help myself, I press, "Why didn't you look at the house when you walked by?"

A frown ghosts her brows before she answers. "Because."

"Because why?"

She sighs. "Because when I woke up this morning, you were gone, and I...I didn't know what to do. I felt," she blows out a breath, "small." The word is so quiet I barely hear it.

But I do. And it breaks my heart.

I roll us over, taking care of the condom before settling myself back between her legs. "Willa Dean Dash," I say softly, "I am not going anywhere."

"That's not true." She whispers it, but she might as well have screamed it into a bullhorn. "You're leaving in two months. Whatever this is…" She trails off.

I close my eyes. I don't know if she's right or not. It's too soon to tell. Never mind the Bunnies being after me. When I open my eyes, she's still staring at me, guileless as always. "I'm not going anywhere for now."

Her throat bobs. "Okay."

And because I'm a selfish asshole, I take her mouth in mine again. A while later, when I slide into her once more, I try not to think about how she feels like home.

CHAPTER 19

WILLA

"YOU GOT LAID." Goldie's eyes are as bright as the morning sun as she takes me in. She grabs my hands and leads me to the counter, knowing full well I should be heading to the kitchen to help Dad prep. "By Reid. And I don't think it's the first time, either. Tell me everything!"

I open my mouth, then reconsider.

"Willllllllaaaaaa," Goldie wheedles, folding her hands together. "Pleeeeeaaaase?"

Oh, who am I kidding? Of course I'm spilling. With the biggest grin of my life on my face, I gush, "Yes I did, and *oh my God, Goldie*, it was the best sex of my life!" I try to keep my voice down on that last part.

Goldie whoops, drawing both Mom and Dad's attention. I wave them off, but know it'll only hold them for a few minutes. "Tell me everything!" she demands again. "Is he as hot under those clothes as it looks?"

I nod like a bobblehead. "He's a freaking fantasy, Goldie. I don't even know how it's my life right now."

"How many times?" Her eyes sparkle.

I blink at her. "Seriously?"

She slams the silverware onto the counter. "Uh, *yeah*, seriously. How else am I supposed to survive the desert that is my own sex life?"

I cringe. "I'm not sure I ever want to think about your sex life, Goldie."

"Fair enough, but also, irrelevant, because I have none." She waves the silverware around once more. "Back to you. How many times did you come?"

...Aaand there's the blush, crawling up my neck to bloom on my cheeks like twin spotlights.

Goldie cackles. "Okay, fine. I truly don't understand why you're such a prude, but I'll leave you alone."

Mom swings over. "What's all the commotion about?"

Goldie snorts a laugh and grabs another set of silverware to roll.

"I hate you," I mutter. To Mom, I do my best to give her a breezy answer. "Oh, nothing big. Just some happy news I was sharing."

"And what am I, chopped liver?" she demands, reaching for the rolled silverware to stash it at the end of the counter. "Don't I deserve to hear the happiness?"

I groan. "Mom, it's not—"

"Tell your mother," Dad demands, pointing a very sharp, very large chef's knife at me. "I don't want to listen to her complain about it later."

I cover my face. "Oh my God," I groan. "How am I related to all of you?"

"Tell me already," Mom prods.

Dad waves a packet of sausages at me. "Just tell her."

Goldie sees the look of combined horror/hilarity on my face and turns to Dad, then back to me.

We howl in unison. "He's waving—" Goldie gasps. "SAUSAGES!"

I slide off the stool, gripping it so that I don't fall to the floor in laughter. "It's…Reid," I manage to say, the giggles coming fast and strong.

"What does Reid have to do with my sausage?" Dad asks. He's dead serious about it, too.

"Sausage," Goldie wheezes, pointing at Dad with one arm and holding her stomach with the other. "What does Reid have to do with *my sausage*, he asks. Oh, *shit*." She meets my eyes, and we fall into laughter once more.

Mom looks at both of us blankly, but I see the minute it dawns on her. "Oh dear," she says, then starts to chuckle. "Dean, sweetie." She turns to Dad, who's got the sausage links unpacked and is literally holding one up to the light to look at it, peering to see if it holds the answer to this mystery. Mom snorts out a laugh. "Dean! Put the sausage down."

"Please," I say, wiping the tears away. "Please, Dad, for the love of all that is holy, put the sausage down."

Dad harrumphs and turns away from all of us, muttering, while we collapse again into a fit of giggles.

After a moment, we manage to gather our composure. Mom exhales. "Well. Wow. Okay." She giggles again, and it nearly sends us off once more, but I manage to hold it in. "You and Reid."

I nod, but the mortification is long gone, thanks to Dad and his sausage links. "Don't get all starry-eyed, Mom," I warn her. "He's not staying."

"Well, of course not," she titters. "But you can leave with him."

"That's not happening," I say flatly.

"Well, you never know," she says. "Plans have a way of changing. It's not the same, of course, but I didn't plan on staying when I came to visit this town, either, and look where we are now."

I raise an eyebrow. "Exactly. You *stayed*." I head to the kitchen to finally join Dad in prep and ignore the noise of protest Mom makes behind me.

Dad slides his gaze over. "You ladies done clucking like a bunch of hens out there?"

"You done pretending like you're a big, strong man who bosses his women around?" I toss back.

He tries to hide his grin, but I catch it. And a minute later, when Mom comes by on her way to the freezer for a new tub of ice cream, I see the way she grabs my dad's butt, too.

It's hard not to admire the way those two love each other. I can't imagine ever having it, but gosh, I'd love to. This thing with Reid, as unbelievable as it is, will only last as long as he's here. When he's gone, he's gone.

So I need to be okay with that and enjoy him while he's here. It's a fling, right? That's what Goldie called it at the very beginning.

But what if I *did* follow him back to Miami?

No. I can't even conceive of it. It's not that I couldn't hack it in a high-end restaurant there, flex my skills and stretch a little. I know I could. And I have Reid to thank for that, in a way, because I wouldn't have dared to even consider the possibility a month ago. But now, I'm realizing that I'm more capable of things. Stronger than I realized. I'm no longer the scared chef-in-training who cried the second Chef Todd turned his ire on me in front of a sea of cameras. I can't quite put my finger on when the change started to happen, but I know it's happened.

The thing about moving is I still don't want to. I love it here, in this little diner a few blocks from the ocean. I love the regulars, the tourists; I even love the way I can't ever get the smell of french fries completely out of my skin. I know a lot of people want to flee where they grew up, and I don't begrudge them that. But this is home.

Later, Reid comes into the diner, all smiles and jokes with

Tom and Jerry while petting the kitten strapped to his chest. He slides onto a stool at the counter and raises those mirrored sunglasses to meet my eyes, popping those stupid dimples as he grins at me.

I'm pretty certain that Reid MacKinnon is going to break my heart. And I can't quite find it in myself to care.

IT'S ANOTHER FIRST FRIDAY, WHICH MEANS IT'S another art bonanza for our sweet little downtown and it's Goldie's turn to drive. The first words out of her mouth as I hop into her Jeep are, "Where's Reid?"

I grin. "Officer MacKinnon is on duty this evening."

"Ooh, so we get to see him in uniform." She wiggles her shoulders as she turns the Jeep around and angles us toward downtown.

I laugh. "We *always* get to see him in uniform," I remind her.

"Yeah, but most of the time you're working, right? Now you can really get your ogle on." She winks at me.

"You really do need to have sex, don't you?"

She raises her water bottle in salute and takes a sip. "Told you. Have you and he done the horizontal mambo since Tuesday?"

I groan. "You're incorrigible."

"I'm *fun*. There's a difference," she corrects. "So? Mambo? Horizontally? Let me live vicariously through you."

"It doesn't creep you out that you're about to get details from your sister?"

She shakes her head. "No. Remember, you're the one with the hang-ups, not me."

I laugh. I have most definitely seen Reid since Tuesday. I saw him Tuesday night, Wednesday night, and last night. We traded houses, each of us taking turns to cook for each other, then having a ridiculous amount of seriously hot sex before passing out in each other's arms. Well, we'd have the hot sex, then he'd get up to check the windows and doors "just to make sure," he said, before tucking me into his side like I was his teddy bear.

Which, for the record, I am delighted to be. He's a great snuggler, and I gotta admit, I did not see that coming.

I also did not see any of this coming, so maybe I'm not the best judge of cuddlers? Anyway.

"Hey, earth to Willa." Goldie's fingers snap in front of my face, pulling me out of my reverie. "Did I lose you to a sea of sexual memories?"

I snort. "Kind of."

She sighs. "Then regale me, woman."

"He's an incredible cook." I give her the details as she drives, keeping the really saucy bits to myself.

Matty's waiting on us at our designated meet-up spot, and as we approach, he does the same move he always does, crooking his arms for both of us to thread ours through. "Ah, the Dash sisters on each arm. How lucky am I?"

"Very," I say.

"Incredibly," Goldie echoes, her voice a bit breathier than it was a few minutes ago.

We turn the corner onto the main stretch of the art walk, and Goldie spies the coffee stand up ahead. "I'm in desperate need of an iced coffee. Anyone else want one?"

I shake my head, and she takes off.

"So, how are things?" Matty asks once she's out of earshot.

I lean into him. "So good. But also, so bad."

"Ah, the ol' *'he's only here for a little while but maybe he'll stay but maybe he won't but maybe you should follow him but you're a strong, independent woman and what would everyone think if you did that'* thing?"

I stare at him. "Who are you, and where did Matty go?"

He laughs and shrugs. "I read too many romances. What can I say?"

"Fair enough. But honestly? That's…kind of it."

He wraps his arm around me, pulling me in tight. "It'll be okay, Wills. Listen your heart."

I snort. "Yeah, well, my heart is telling me it just wants more of that D."

Matty stops dead in his tracks, pulling me around to face him so I can't miss his shocked expression. "Did you just make an actual reference to sex?"

I cover my own mouth, just as shocked that I said it. "Um, yeah?"

He shakes his head. "I'm not sure how I feel about this. But also, is it okay if I ask that you never do that again? I may be your best friend, but I'm also a guy, and it turns out that I am not okay with hearing that you want some 'D'." He throws air quotes.

I nod. "I blame Goldie."

"Blame me for what?" she asks, returning with an iced latte for herself and a black coffee for Matty.

He takes it. "How'd you know I really wanted one?"

She eyes him. "I pay attention, Matty. It's not hard. What am I being blamed for?"

"Her suddenly dirty mouth."

"And here I was giving her crap for not being dirty *enough*," Goldie jokes as we continue down the street.

Vendors are set up like always, the art beautiful in the slowly setting sun. A breeze floats from the ocean, tinging everything with a salty air, and I inhale happily. I may be confused, but at least I have my sister and best friend in the most amazing town I could hope for.

Someone yells my name. "I was hoping I'd see you all," Agatha says. "Matty, do you still do house calls? My daughter

Jessica's dog is having some trouble getting used to the baby and I'm sure you'd have some good insight."

Jessica herself comes up behind her mother, pushing a stroller. Plenty of oohs and ahhs abound, until Goldie is pulling the baby out and holding her against her chest, cooing and bouncing like it's the most normal thing in the world.

My neck tingles, and sure enough, Reid and Ox are heading our way. We widen the circle and Reid's hand comes to rest on my lower back. He leans down to whisper in my ear. "Hey, you."

I smile up at him, goosebumps tingling in the wake of his touch. "Hi."

Jessica interrupts. "So, you're the temp they brought in to keep my spot warm," she jokes, holding a hand out to Reid.

He takes it. "Yes, ma'am. You must be Jessica."

"And you're Chief's nephew," she finishes.

"Also known as Reid," Ox says.

Jessica takes her daughter from Goldie and bounces her. "You think you might wanna stick around, Reid? This motherhood thing has thrown me a bit and I'm thinking about going part time. I bet Chief would be open to keeping you."

My stupid, stupid heart absolutely soars at the words. I push the thought down, because it's too much to hope for. Two months of Reid and his dimples. That's all I get.

"Too soon for that kind of conversation," Reid hedges, his eyes sliding to mine for the briefest of moments as he speaks.

My heart flares again.

"Wanna hold her?" Jessica asks. "I hear you're usually walking around with a cat, but since the cat isn't around…"

"I'm not the greatest with babies," Reid starts, but it's too late, because Jessica's already plopped the baby in his arms. He's hilariously uncomfortable, going stiff as a board and as still as possible, and he looks like he's somewhere between horror and awe as he regards the tiny package.

Matty laughs. "You're making the rest of us guys look really bad, Reid."

Ox crosses his arms thoughtfully. "I don't know. She's not crying, so it's a win in my book."

As if on cue, the baby breaks into a howl. Reid startles, and Jessica lunges to grab her daughter.

"Is that sweat on your brow?" Ox asks, peering closer at Reid.

"Don't ever let me hold a baby again," he says to a chorus of laughter.

Jessica and Agatha move away and Reid turns to me. "You enjoying yourself?"

I smile. "We've barely gotten started, but yeah. You? How's your first First Friday Art Walk shift going? Any nefarious activities I should be on the lookout for?" I tease.

He grins, one of his dimples popping out as he does. Ugh, why does he have to be so *cute*? "Not yet, but it's early. Gotta watch out—when the sun goes down is when the riffraff comes out."

I laugh, then yelp as someone knocks me from behind. As I flail forward, grabbing Reid for balance, the guy keeps walking without a backward glance.

Reid gets me upright, then his hand flies to his holster as he turns to watch the man. "Are you okay?" he asks, turning back to rake his glance over me.

"I'm fine, Reid." But my voice is shaky. Reid turned into a different person right in front of my eyes. "It was an accident."

"Ox." Reid's voice brooks no dissent.

Ox nods, and Reid takes off, jogging in the direction of the man who seems to have disappeared into the crowd.

"It wasn't a big deal," I tell Ox, but he shakes his head.

"Don't assume you know everything about him, Willa."

His words send chills down my spine. "What...what do you mean?"

He presses his lips together. "That's not something I can talk about. But trust that if Reid says it's a problem, then it's a problem."

After a beat, Matty says, "On that note, why don't we all keep going? I'd really like to see the new, uh, spoon maker."

Ox nods at us. "Be careful." His tone is far more serious than I've ever heard, and it sends a chill down my spine.

I don't see Reid anywhere after that, and I can't shake the sense of unease that clings to me for the rest of the night.

Later that night, after I'm already in bed, there's a loud banging on my door. I squeak out a yelp and bury myself under the covers, my heart leaping into my throat. That's a big nope for me, thanks. No one is home.

Then the door opens, and I scramble to sit up on the bed, pulling the blankets around me as though they're somehow going to help.

"Willa?" His voice is tense and tight.

I sag with relief. "Reid?"

He's in the bedroom in a few strides, still in his uniform, his hand hovering over his gun. "I repeatedly tell you to lock the door," he growls. "Especially after what happened tonight, and you still didn't do it? What is wrong with you?"

I gape up at him, my heart right back to pounding. "I…I forgot. I've just never"

"You. Can't. Forget," he says, his eyes almost wild in the dim of the bedroom. "Your life may one day depend on it."

I turn on the bedside lamp, needing to shed actual light on the situation. "Reid, we live…*I* live," I correct, "in a tiny little beach town. Aside from some petty crime here and there, there's nothing to worry about."

He clenches his jaw and looks away. "That's not true, Willa."

"I get that you're from the big city, Reid, but honestly, this is a safe town. Maybe you're just seeing things that aren't there."

His eyes flash. "You don't know me nearly well enough to say that sort of thing, Willa."

My mouth pops open, and he seems to deflate before my eyes.

"There are things you don't know. That you *can't* know, for your own safety." He runs his hand through his hair and blows out a breath, turning in a circle.

He looks so pained that my heart twists for him. "I'm sorry," I whisper.

He hangs his head. "You don't have anything to apologize for." He raises his eyes to mine. "Just promise me you'll lock your door? Be more alert?"

I nod, the creeping sense of unease from earlier tonight settling back around my shoulders. "Okay."

He looks around. "Where's Midnight?"

I smile softly. "She's in her bed over here."

He nods, then lets out a breath, seeming to come to a decision as his beautiful green eyes meet mine again. "Can I...can I stay here tonight?"

"Of course."

"Be right back." He leaves, then returns five minutes later with a change of clothes. "Mind if I shower here?"

Afterward, he pulls his service weapon out of its holster and places it on the bedside table. "It's a precautionary measure," he says, his voice soft.

"Reid..." But the pained expression on his face wipes away anything I was going to say.

He climbs into the bed and wraps his bulk around mine, the warmest security blanket on the planet. He kisses my shoulder, and another exhale leaves him as he finally relaxes.

I turn in his arms to study him. Something is obviously wrong. "Are you okay?"

His expression is pained. "No."

I pause. "Can you talk about it?"

"No," he repeats.

It shouldn't hurt my feelings as much as it does, but his answer cleaves me in two. I try again. "Did you find the guy you were looking for? The one who ran into me?" He shakes his head, seeming so haunted that I ask, "Do you need to be the little spoon?" I'm half joking, but when he nods, I don't hesitate. "Turn over," I tell him.

I wrap myself around him, kissing the smooth skin of his back and taking in his cedar and honey smell. After a while, his breathing evens out. Only then do I let myself fall asleep.

REID

T'S BEEN THREE days since someone bumped into Willa, and I can't shake the feeling that it's got something to do with the Bunnies. How could it not? I spent the weekend upgrading my existing security system and expanding it to encompass Willa's place, getting Agatha's permission to do it on hers as well. I've got a live feed that constantly pushes to my phone, and I'm not proud of how much I've been checking it.

I've never been like this. The entire time I was undercover with the Bunnies, I was calm. I understood the risks, and I was willing to take them.

But here? With Willa? I'm entirely unprepared for whatever this is. It's suffocating, the constant worry. I can't get a full breath and I'm entirely on edge. I need it to stop.

My shoes squelch as I run along the beach. I've not been on sand since leaving Miami, and I don't know why I stopped, but my calves are screaming about it right now. After logging a mile on the torturous stuff, I turn up the access path and aim toward home, speeding up in an effort to get everything out of my head. Just focus on the run.

I'm out of breath and nearly ready to die by the time I arrive home. Slowing to a walk, my eyes land on something glinting on my doorknob.

I look around, checking up and down the street, looking for anything out of the ordinary.

Nothing.

Approaching my door, my gut clenches. It's a white rabbit's foot.

The Bunnies have been here.

My heart climbs into my throat, and spikes erupt inside my chest. It takes everything I have not to scream in frustration.

Stepping into the house, I pull up the security feeds, but of course, I see nothing. The Bunnies aren't amateurs. I curse and punch the button to call my chief in Miami.

"MacKinnon." His voice is gruff as he answers.

I don't bother with niceties. "They've left their calling card on my front door."

"Shit."

"Anything you can do from there?"

A sigh comes through the phone. "You know as well as I do that you're out of my jurisdiction. You're on your own over there, Mac."

My jaw ticks. "I figured. What about off the books? Anything?"

"Doubtful. I'll alert the DA, but you know they won't do shit over there."

"Anything will help."

"You good, MacKinnon? You don't sound like your usual self."

"I'm good," I lie. "Just wasn't expecting a rabbit's foot on my front door."

He grunts. "Going from the deliverer to the receiver."

"Exactly." Even though I'd never seen the results, I'd been the messenger of doom for the Bunnies more than my fair share of times when I was undercover.

"Stay alert."

"Will do," I respond. We hang up, and I get ready for work. I stop by Betty's desk at the station, asking her if she's noticed anything out of the ordinary and telling her to be on the lookout.

She gives me a look. "Everything all right, Reid?"

What is it with the perceptive women in this town? But I give her what I hope is a convincing smile. "Of course. Just let me know if you hear of anything unusual?"

"Sure thing."

My uncle has the same reaction as Chief Muñoz when I deliver him the news. "Shit."

"Have you told anyone else?"

"Course not," he scoffs. "You said we needed to keep this contained. Have you?"

"Not exactly," I hedge.

"Not exactly? What does that mean?" His eyes narrow.

"Ox is a really good cop, you know that?" I say instead.

He huffs. "He is. But whatever he does or doesn't know is on you, son. Not me."

"Understood."

"You're on duty with Thompson today."

I nod, not happy to be paired with the guy but knowing better than to argue about it, and leave him to it.

Officer Ted Thompson is no more a fan of me than I am of him, and he flicks his eyes at me dismissively when I join him at the front of the station. "Stuck with each other today?"

I don't bother answering, moving to open the door and gesturing for him to go in front of me. He makes a sound of disgust, and the flare of anger that swells inside me takes me by surprise.

We head to the pier, with Thompson naturally choosing to drive the short distance instead of walking. He's the exact type of cop that gives the rest of us a bad name, and between the rabbit's foot this morning and my need to be one step ahead of his surly attitude, my nerves are shot. I leap out of the car the second he puts it in park, filling my lungs with the salty ocean breeze. I clock everything around me: the young teenagers who bounce and jostle each other as they head toward the shake and burger shack on the corner, the number and type of vessels out in the water, the old man who sits and reads the paper outside of the bait and tackle shop just off the front of the pier, the joggers, the moms with strollers. No hint of anyone who'd be with the Bunnies.

Everything is cataloged and filed before Thompson heaves his bulk out of the front seat and joins me, his hands resting on his utility belt and surveying the pier as if he rules over it. He starts for the teenagers. "Looks like we have our work cut out for us."

I block him, my arms deliberately loose.

"What are you doing?"

"Please tell me why you think you need to talk to those kids."

His eyes flash. "I don't have to explain myself to you, MacKinnon."

"Give me one good reason to speak to them," I repeat. This asshole has no idea what I've experienced in Miami, and I am not dealing with his racist ass today.

His eyes, bloodshot and beady, flit between mine as he considers my words. Finally, he huffs and turns in the direction of the pier. I know he plans to ticket as many people as possible, but I'll take a handful of twenty-dollar fines over harassing kids for their skin color any fucking day of the week.

Sure enough, Thompson has a grand old time, his enjoyment over ticketing tourists for not having the proper license growing with each one he issues. But after he writes the fifth citation in as many people as he's asked, I'm done. "What is it with you?"

He turns to me, his expression dangerous. "Me? What is it with *you*?"

"They're here to relax, Thompson, not trying to wipe the pier of fish. What's your deal?"

He shrugs. "There are signs everywhere. The license is three dollars. They need to learn their lesson."

I clench my jaw, knowing I should let it go. Arguing with partners—temporary or not, racist assholes or not—puts a target on my back if something goes wrong.

He smirks. "That's what I thought."

Well, fuck him then. "Only lesson they're learning is that you're a petty prick, and you're making the rest of us look like pricks right alongside you."

He laughs, entirely too pleased to have gotten a rise out of me. Then he leans forward and lowers his voice. "Listen up, you little shit. I don't like you. Coming here from your big city thinking you're hot stuff when it's easy enough to see you couldn't do a real policeman's job if your life fucking depended on it. You're slow to react, you probably couldn't hit a target even if it were served up to you on a platter, and your observational skills are worse than a blind man's."

The urge to throat-punch the asshole is high, but I hide it, crossing my arms and regarding him coolly. "You're a real treat, you know that?"

His ruddy cheeks get redder. "We're done here."

"Pretty sure you don't need a partner to harass the tourists. I'll finish my shift alone." I pivot and walk away, already knowing I've behaved rashly and unable to give a shit.

He mutters a few words behind me that I don't catch, but I keep going. If I spend another minute in his company, I'm liable to do something I'll regret.

CHAPTER 21

WILLA

S O IT TURNS out that I am a horn dog.

Horn. Dog.

That's the only way I can accurately be described at this point. At the end of the day, it's Reid's fault. The man is a walking fantasy with his skin and his muscles and his beard and his eyes and dimples and mouth. He's orgasmed me into a state of I don't even know what, but I'm so happy about it that I can't be bothered to care about his inevitable departure. I know he's leaving, but my body is so addicted to his that it's overriding all logic. I spend all day thinking of him, and I blame all the orgasms for the things that go through my mind.

Things like, will he let me use his cuffs? Probably not. And that's why I've gotten a pair off Amazon and they're in my bedside drawer.

Mom and Goldie don't help matters, because they won't shut up about me and Reid, despite me and Dad begging them to stop.

"Maybe you'll go to Miami." Mom pours Tom and Jerry more coffee.

"That girl's not going anywhere," Tom says.

"That girl can do what she wants, Tom," Jerry shoots back.

"That girl is right here, guys," I call through the window. It's slow, so I'm tidying up the area where we garnish all the plates. "And I've said it a million times: I am not going anywhere."

"But you could be so much bigger if you left," Mom wheedles. "You need to leave. Explore. Discover the world. Discover yourself."

"Barbara, leave her alone," Dad says. "You act like you don't want her around."

I shoot him a grateful look as Mom sniffs, "I just think this town is too small for our Willa."

"I like it here," I insist.

"Because Reid is here?" Tom waggles his eyes.

I glare at him. "Not you, too."

"Everyone can see how moony-eyed you get when he comes in," Jerry points out.

I roll my eyes. "I give up. All of you can think what you want. I'm staying here. I'm not following Reid—or *anyone*—anywhere."

"If you say so," Mom singsongs.

I ignore her. There's no talking her out of anything when she gets something in her head, and she's convinced herself that Reid and I are going to live happily ever after in Miami. Then again, she's been trying to push me out of town from the moment I graduated from high school, so I shouldn't be surprised.

I go home after my shift, knowing full well that Reid's waiting in his backyard for me, like most days. But I have plans for him, plans that I'm not sure I'll even have the bravery to pull off, but I want to try anyway. So I ignore him and walk into my house, deliberately leaving the door unlocked and dropping a trail of clothes in my wake as I head to the shower.

I half expect him to join me, but he doesn't. Instead, he's waiting on the edge of my bed again, scowling, and it sends my heart rate soaring. I smirk to cover my nervousness. "You're awfully cute when you're mad, Reid."

He's unmoved. "Willa, you have *got* to lock your door."

I sigh and let my towel drop. His eyes go right to my breasts. "I knew you were coming," I say, closing the distance between us and stepping between his legs, hoping the move will keep my own from shaking. "Otherwise, I assure you I would have."

His hands skim up the backs of my legs, over my rear, and make their way to my waist. He pulls me close and presses his lips to my stomach. "Promise?" he asks, not breaking the contact.

Relaxing and reminding myself that he's damn near perfect and will not, in fact, make fun of me, I thread my nails across his scalp the way I know he likes it. "Promise." I reach to pull his shirt off. He lets me, then he lets me take his shorts and boxer briefs off as well. His dick is already half-hard. "You're being awfully compliant, Officer Reid," I tease.

He smiles, seeming to have pushed whatever was bothering him to the side. "I kind of like it when you take control."

I bite my lip and breathe deeply through my nose. *I can do this.* "What do you think about letting me do something?"

He raises a brow, intrigued. "Like what?"

I crawl up the bed, hoping I don't look like an absolute fool, and reach into the bedside drawer. *Now or never, Willa. Be brave.* I pull the cuffs out and brandish them. "Let me cuff you?"

He chuckles indulgently. "This from the woman who I had to force to say 'cock' the first time we had sex."

My cheeks redden as I smile, trying hard to fight the shyness that threatens to overtake me. "This is all your fault, Reid. What do you think?"

He slides up to meet me at the head of the mattress, then cups my cheek and kisses me. "For you, Willa—anything."

I grin and open them, leaning over his chest to cuff one wrist to the bedpost I never knew I'd be so delighted to have.

He raises and captures my nipple in his mouth, and I hiss in surprised pleasure, then let myself sink into it.

"That feels good," I moan.

He hums and continues his work, threading his leg through mine and pulling me onto him.

But I won't be deterred. With far more willpower than I knew I had, I lift myself off and grab his other wrist, pulling it toward his other and forcing him into an angle on the bed.

When I close the second cuff around him, he winces.

"Did I hurt you?"

"No," he says, "But put the key on the bedside table for me. I need to see you do it."

I grin. "Willing to let me control you...within reason. You got it, Officer MacKinnon."

Just as I knew it would, the phrase lights him up. I place the keys where he asked, then rise to consider the gorgeous man below me. Then I descend, kissing him with abandon and letting my hands roam over his flawless body. I still avoid the gunshot wound; I can't quite bring myself to get near it, despite it being entirely healed.

Reid's kisses are drugging, controlling me even when I'm the one in control. The way his tongue glides against mine, the promise of more to come, it's intoxicating. I manage to wrench my lips from his, kissing a trail down his neck to his powerful chest and skimming my teeth against one nipple, then the next, exactly how he likes it. He inhales sharply above me as I start to descend lower, spending time on his flat, firm stomach. He's not sporting a six-pack, but it's toned and sexy as hell, with a delightful line of dark hair leading down.

"You have the prettiest dick, Reid," I tell him as I settle between his thighs.

He chuckles. "If you say so, gorgeous."

I lean down and bite the inside of his thigh, eliciting a hiss that quickly turns into a groan. "I say so." Then, because I want to know what it feels like, I use the words he did with me the first time. "Eyes on me, Reid."

He locks onto me, his pupils blown with desire.

I smile, then lick him from root to tip, taking immense pleasure in the way his eyes roll back into his head before snapping back to mine. Then I swirl my tongue around the tip, tasting the salty precum and moaning. Reid groans in response.

"Tell me something, Officer." My heart is beating far too fast. "Do you like it when I lick you?" I lick him up and down slowly. "Or when I suck you?" I pull him into my throat, angling my body up so I can get as much of him into my mouth as possible. I'm nowhere near that whole "swallowing the tip" thing and never will be, but that's why I have hands.

Reid groans unintelligibly above me, his hips bucking into me as I suck. I release him with a pop and grin up at him. "Which is it?"

He growls. "Suck me, Willa."

I lick my lips, a bolt of desire streaking through me. "God, that's hot."

"You have no fucking idea," he answers, then moans as I take him into my mouth again.

I give him exactly what he wants, and even though I'm the one on my knees, it's the most powerful I've ever felt. Because I'm the one with his balls in my hand. I'm the one controlling his pleasure. I'm the one who's taking him to the edge and pulling back. I'm the one who's reduced him to a quivering mess below me.

"Fuck, Willa—I'm gonna come," he growls.

I pop off him and pull my hands away.

"Fuck!" His eyes are wild with lust. "You're going to pay for this, Willa."

I preen. "I thought you said you liked being edged."

He heaves a shuddering sigh and grits out, "I did."

"Then what are you going to do to me, Officer?"

He narrows his eyes, his breath coming in pants. "Guess you'll find out."

"Is that a promise?" I crawl up his body, then lower myself so that his dick is almost touching my pussy. "Do you want to fuck me, Reid?"

He nods. "I do."

"Do you want to come first?"

He shakes his head.

"Too bad." And with that, I move down and suck him again, moaning against him as he yells above me.

When he tenses for what might be the fifth time, I keep going. Then I pop off and pump him, letting the ropes of his release fly onto his stomach, my eyes locked on his as he comes. When he finishes, he goes limp and closes his eyes. "Fuck me, Willa," he murmurs. "You're a fucking beast."

I grin, more than a little satisfied with myself. "Stay there."

"Kind of can't move, sweetheart."

"Oh yeah," I giggle, then hop off the bed to get him a warm washcloth. Returning, I clean him and barely have the cuffs off before he snaps, tossing me onto the mattress and pinning me down.

I suck in a startled breath.

"I told you you'd pay for that, sweet Willa," he growls, and his voice is full of sinful promise. "Did you not believe me?"

I shake my head. "I believed you."

"Good. Now, find something to hold onto, because I'm going to make you scream."

Fuck.

He lowers himself to between my legs and thrusts his fingers inside me without warning.

"Fuck!" I scream. Literally *scream*.

"That's right, Willa," he says, then licks the sensitive bundle of nerves as he pumps his fingers in and out. "You're going to come fast and hard." Then he sucks at me, snaking his other hand up to pinch my nipple. The pain is sharp and intense, but the pleasure from his mouth and fingers overrides the sensation.

I buck against his face, and in moments, he's wrung an orgasm out of me, quick, hot, and bright.

"One." His voice is low and dangerous.

I blow out a breath. "This isn't the punishment you think it is."

He doesn't answer, just flips me over and smacks one of my butt cheeks. *Hard.*

"Ow!" I squeal. "Jesus!"

"That's not my name, Willa." He smacks the other side.

"Reid!" I hustle to say, then repeat it. "Fuck," I moan, because now he's yanked my hips up and is licking me from behind, the sting of the spanks already forgotten. I circle my hips, and he pulls away, planting another smack on my ass, then soothing it with slow, gentle circles of his palm.

"I told you that you'd pay for teasing me, Willa." His voice is deep, animalistic. He licks me. "Did you think I was kidding?"

He rises. Another smack, followed by another warm palm rubbing at the sting. My heart races, and sweat beads on my brow. I think I like this.

Behind me, I hear the tearing of a foil. How is he hard again already? In seconds, the tip of him enters me.

I groan and push back against him, desperate to have him seated in me.

He pulls out, then pushes a finger inside instead. He leans his chest against my back, his breath hot against my neck.

"You want my cock, Willa?"

I whimper.

"You can't have it. You're not even close to getting it."

I moan. "I'm sorry, Reid." Another smack of his palm against my ass. "I'm sorry, Officer." Another. I grip the sheets, spiraling into a completely different world. "Officer," I breathe. "I'm sorry for teasing you, *Officer.*"

He gives me the tip of his dick again, rubbing it against my clit and sliding it between my folds to tease my opening. "No," he murmurs darkly. "I think I need a better apology than that." He pushes between my shoulder blades to force me onto the mattress, then hops off the bed. He grabs the cuffs and dangles them in front of me. "Your turn." My arms are pinned behind my back and secured at the base of my spine before I can even take a full breath.

"Fuck." My voice hitches, and I try to calm my racing heart.

He leans down and gently turns my chin so our eyes meet. "Are they too tight?"

"N-no," I stammer.

"Good. You remember your safe word?"

I blink. "Safe word?"

He grins sweetly, then kisses my forehead. "Yes, sweet girl. Last time, it was avocado. You choosing that again?"

I don't appreciate the way my heart squeezes at his thoughtfulness. "Yes," I whisper.

His eyes darken, and he clenches his teeth. "Good."

With that, Considerate Reid is gone, replaced once more by the sex god I've unwittingly unleashed into the bedroom.

He keeps me on my stomach, nipping and biting at my shoulders, then soothing them with his tongue. He shoves a palm beneath me to grab my breast, squeezing hard.

"I fucking love these tits, Willa," he growls. "And one day I'm going to fuck them. Come all over them. Paint a goddamn Pollock on them and then make you lick what's left off my cock."

Thrills of pleasure shoot through me. "Yes," I hiss. Because I want it just as badly as he does.

He slides his palm down my belly, then gets to my pussy. He palms it, squeezing. The pressure is both pain and bliss, and I moan.

"In here, this is mine."

I nod.

He squeezes harder. "Out there, this is mine."

I nod again, forcing air into my lungs.

"You are mine, Willa. Make no fucking mistake about it. Your pussy. Your sassy little mouth. Your body, *fuck me*, your body." He rubs his forehead and face against my back, as if he's marking me with his scent. "Drive me fucking crazy with this body."

I writhe beneath him. "Reid," I breathe. "I need…"

His laugh is dangerous. "I don't care what you need right now, Willa." He moves his palm from my pussy and squeezes my hip, then my ass. He spreads my butt cheeks and runs his dick between them. "You ever been fucked here, sweet girl?"

I shake my head.

"This ass is mine, too. And one day, I'll fuck this ass, and you'll scream my name as I pound into it. Do you understand?"

Whether I want it or not isn't a question right now. That much is clear. I nod.

He pushes a thumb against the hole back there, and I clench against him. He smacks my butt with his free hand. "Relax."

I force myself to do as he commands, and he pulls his thumb away. I heave out a breath, then inhale sharply as he shoves his fingers into my pussy. "Fuuuuuck," I moan. The sound is guttural. But he pulls his fingers out immediately, and I whine.

He flips me over and takes a breast into his mouth, then the other, his fingers working my clit the entire time.

"I'm—" But I can't finish, because the orgasm is cresting from nowhere, wracking my body as he sucks on my nipple and works my clit.

"Two."

He pulls away when I come down, kneeling before me and pumping his dick. I watch hungrily.

"You like watching me fuck my hand, Willa?"

I nod and lick my lips. "I do." My hips swirl involuntarily, aching with emptiness. "I need it, Reid."

He smirks. "I know." Standing, he yanks me to the edge of the mattress and turns me over again. He takes a moment to massage my arms and shoulders, releasing the tension that's built there from being in cuffs. "I'm going to stand you up now."

I barely register what he's doing before I'm up and being walked to the wall. It's hot as hell, but it feels like one wrong move would have me punished.

"Stay still," he commands.

I obey. My cheek is pressed against the cool plaster, as is my chest and belly.

"Spread your legs for me, gorgeous."

I do it.

"Tell me, Willa. Have you ever been fucked standing up?"

I swallow. "No," I croak.

"Have you ever been fucked wearing cuffs?"

"No."

"Do you want the cuffs off?"

"I want whatever you want," I respond.

"Good answer," he praises. "You're a fast learner. And for that, you get your reward."

His hands, warm and calloused, are on mine as he unlocks the cuffs and tosses them on the floor. Without warning, he lines himself up and thrusts in.

"Oh my God, thank you so much," I moan, writhing against him. "Thank you, thank you, thank you."

"You want all of this cock, Willa?" His mouth is against my ear, sending shivers as he speaks.

"Please," I whisper.

He pulls back and pushes in again, going deeper this time.

"Yessss," I hiss, my eyes rolling back in my head with the pleasure of it.

"There we go," he murmurs, one hand reaching to grab my breast while another goes to my clit and circles it.

"Spread your arms."

I do as he commands, and then he snaps, pounding into me.

"Yes, yes, *yes*, Reid, oh please don't stop, please, please,

please," I chant, unable to do anything but take it as he thrusts into me over and over.

He pulls out and turns me around, and I meet his eyes for the first time in what feels like hours. It's like coming home. The green depths are unfathomable, swirling with lust and something else. There's a part of him I can't reach right now, something dark and feral, but it doesn't scare me.

"Give it to me, Reid," I say, finally brave enough to take whatever darkness he has. "I want it."

His eyes flash. "Jump."

I do it, wrapping my legs around his hips as he pushes back into me. We groan in unison as he locks us into position, my back against the wall, my heels digging into the top of his ass, as he pounds into me.

It's not pretty. It's not romantic. It's animalistic and angry and brutal and I. Love. Every. Bit. Of. It. "More," I urge, my breath coming in hot pants. "Give me more."

He growls, his palms gripping my shoulders for leverage as he thrusts in.

"More, Reid!"

"Fuck!" he yells, turning and dropping me onto the bed. "Turn over. All fours. Now."

I do it as he lowers himself to his knees. He slides in. "Chest down."

I obey once again and am rewarded as he yanks my hips to his, his fingers pressing into my flesh so hard that I'm bound to have bruises.

The orgasm builds slowly this time, coming from deep inside me. "Reid," I groan, my voice something I don't even recognize. "I need this, need you, don't stop."

"Fuck, Willa, you're everything," he pants behind me. "So tight. Come for me, baby. I need you to come."

I feel my walls start to clench, and I give myself over. The pleasure crests as I yell into the mattress, unable to do anything but sob that I'm coming as his grip tightens even further, his own orgasm hitting him right along with mine.

He roars behind me, pounding faster and faster, then stilling as he throbs inside me.

We breathe.

I release my grip on the sheets.

His forehead touches my back, then he kisses my spine as he pulls out. I collapse onto the bed as he disposes of the condom. When he returns, he flops beside me, yanking me blindly to him and squeezing me tight.

Somewhere along the line, it felt like he was fighting some demons I couldn't see, but it doesn't matter. Because I have my Reid back now.

I almost stop breathing.

My Reid?

No. He's not mine. And never will be.

I swallow the lump in my throat as he rains kisses on my shoulder.

Chapter 22

Reid

T HERE'S ANOTHER RABBIT'S foot on my doorknob after my run on Friday, the white of it almost blending into the door.

I slow to a deliberate walk, checking my surroundings for clues I know won't be around as the high I'd been on dissolves into frustration and anger. I bag the foot even though I know there won't be fingerprints, then pull up my phone to check the camera feed. The asshole is good. Professional. Covered head to toe except for the eyes, and they don't so much as glance in any camera's direction.

Fuck.

My gut twists. It's bad enough that he's been at my house, but even worse is that Willa, innocent and completely unaware of the danger she's in by virtue of being connected to me, was sleeping in her own place not thirty yards away.

I get ready for work, then meet Willa to grab Midnight as she's leaving for her shift. I lean down for a kiss. "Isn't this better than using Agatha's car as a hiding spot from me?"

She reddens. "You saw that?"

I chuckle, the adorableness of her blush calming me a little as

I tuck a strand of hair behind her ear. "Willa. I saw everything. Including your beautiful tits that first day you undressed in your house when I was in my backyard."

She shoves at me playfully. "Rude."

I hold my hands up. "It wasn't on purpose, I swear! How was I supposed to know you were giving strip shows to your neighbors on the daily?"

She twists her lips. "Uh-huh."

We walk to our separate cars and she gives Midnight a scratch beneath her chin. The kitten launches her motor purr. "See you later?"

I grin. "Of course." As I turn away, she calls my name. I look back.

"You okay?"

Damn this woman and her perceptiveness. "I'm good."

She's unconvinced, that much is clear, but she nods and smiles at me anyway.

I'm on patrol with Ox today and am far too distracted, my thoughts swinging between the Bunnies and Willa. The Bunnies, who clearly know I'm here and are letting me know they're days from trying to kill me, and Willa, sweet Willa, who I'm more anxious about the Bunnies getting to than me.

It's honestly more concerning that they *haven't* targeted her. I'm missing something critical in this entire thing. Like there's a thread dangling in front of me that I just can't grab.

Ox and I leave the coffee shop with today's haul: lemon poppyseed muffins and a special blend dark roast that is killer with a splash of vanilla cream, when he says, "Okay, man. Spill it."

I look up from giving Midnight a crumb of muffin. "Spill what?"

"Spill what's got you so oblivious to literally everything except whatever's right in front of your face. And don't tell me it's Willa. It's more than that. What's going on with the Bunnies?"

I sigh heavily. "I told Chief Mac you were too smart for your own good."

He grins. "That's why I'll be the next Chief. But seriously. What is it?"

"You know I can't tell you, Ox. It's bad enough you got the fact that I was undercover with them out of me."

He snickers. "I'm good. What can I say?"

I roll my eyes. "The less you know—the less *everyone* knows—the better."

He finishes off his muffin. "You and I are both aware that's complete bullshit, but if you want to play pretend, then fine. We'll do that."

I don't get even a second's worth of relief, though, because his next sentence is, "So, how are things with Willa?"

"You are such an asshole, you know that?"

He laughs. "Pretty sure you've called me that before."

"Willa's...she's great," I admit.

He turns a shit-eating grin on me. "Yeah?"

"You are the *worst*," I huff. "Yeah. She's great. And I'm the asshole who's leaving soon."

"You could stay, you know."

We turn toward the pier. "Nah." I wave the thought away, even though I've considered it more than I should.

"Why not?" Ox asks, his eyes sweeping the surrounding scene. I gotta hand it to him; he does not behave like a small-town cop. Then again, it's been clear since I got here that I have no clue what it means to be a small-town cop, anyway.

"Because I'm a fill-in. No one wants me here permanently."

"Says who? Because Chief Mac seems awfully happy these days, and that's a damn miracle."

"Thompson is not my fan."

"He's not a fan of anyone. Besides, he's a prick."

I snort. "Glad to know I'm not the only one."

He shrugs. "He's been an ass my whole life. Well, I take that back. He was fine until I came out. Then he turned into a bigoted prick. Though I guess he was always a bigoted prick; he just hid it."

"You're gay?" I can't hide the surprise in my voice.

"Uh, yeah man. No one told you?"

"No, but also, it's not their business to tell *your* business."

Ox chuckles. "You're clearly not used to living in a small town."

"Maybe not." I realize I'm not acting any better than Thompson. I stop, and Ox turns. "I'm sorry. I shouldn't be so surprised. I'm from Miami. I know better."

His face softens. "It's good, Reid. But you really gotta drop the whole 'I'm from Miami' thing. You sound like a douche."

I laugh and give Midnight a pet. "Fair enough."

Betty's voice comes through the radio clipped to Ox's shoulder. "Break in over on Pier Boulevard. Short-term rental."

Ox sighs. "Here I was thinking we were going to have a quiet shift." He presses the button. "We're on it, Betty. What's the address?"

"4450."

"10-4."

We hustle to the car, and Ox hops in the driver's seat and punches the ignition on with far more force than usual.

"You gonna throw the lights on, too, little buddy?" I joke.

He shoots me a glare as he hits the gas. "Shut up."

The owner, a man in his mid-sixties or so with pale skin and a look of utter bewilderment, is in the front yard when we get there, wringing his hands.

"Evening, Jesse," Ox says, sticking his hand out for a shake.

Jesse takes it, then swings his glance to me. "This the new guy?"

"Officer Reid MacKinnon." I shake his hand. "Tell us what happened."

He pulls his ball cap off and wrings it. "To be honest, guys,

I'm not even sure that 'break in' is what's been happening. I think I've had a squatter."

"Wanna let us in to take a look around?" Ox asks.

Jesse leads us to the front and opens the door for us. I scan the living room. It's a standard beach rental, decked out in white and pale blue with framed beach art on the walls. "What made you think you've had someone here?"

"Bathroom," he scoffs. "Squatter can't hit the toilet for shit."

Ox huffs a laugh. "Fair enough. Let us check it out, okay? You stay outside."

We step inside and Ox shoots me a look. "What are you thinking?"

"You mean besides wondering how a grown-ass man misses the toilet?"

He snorts.

"Is this normal?"

"Squatters? Nah. Especially right now, when the season is still pretty high. I'm surprised Jesse didn't have this place rented out."

We go through the motions, but after a while, I know it's a dead end. This is where my Bunny hitman has been staying.

"Ox."

He glances over. "Yeah?"

"We're not going to find anything. No prints, no nothing. Nothing's gonna be missing, either."

He stops and looks at me, assessing. "And how would you know that, MacKinnon?"

"Because I know who's been here. Well," I hedge, "not the exact person, but I know why they're here."

"And are you going to share that information with me?"

I shake my head sadly. "No."

"Come on, Reid." He blows out an exasperated sigh. "How am I supposed to do my job, man?"

I hold my hands up. "I know. I'll tell Chief."

"You better," he grumbles, pulling off his gloves and

muttering under his breath. "And you get to be the one to talk to Jesse. *And* file the paperwork."

I gesture for him to exit before me. "That's fair."

Later, after I'm back on patrol on my second shift of the day, I pull over to text Willa.

> Did you lock your doors?

WILLA
> I swear, your obsession with locked doors is unhealthy.

> I mean it, Willa.

WILLA
> You gonna punish me if you come home over and find it's unlocked?

> I'm not joking.

WILLA
> I'm huffing.

> I'm serious.

WILLA
> Hang on.
> Okay, the door is locked. Happy now?

> Very.

Chapter 23

Willa

I HAVEN'T WAITED tables in a good six weeks—not since I first met Reid, come to think of it—but I'm out front again today. Goldie's out of town and it's September, so things are on their way back toward off-season busy instead of insane summer busy. Happily, we're never fully quiet here at the diner, and that's just how I like it. The busier the better, actually.

Except when I'm waiting tables. And then, I'll take a desert. I don't understand how people can just walk around with a tray full of food or drinks and simply...not drop them. Like, how is that possible?

And yet, it's possible for everyone except me.

We're in the middle of the lunch rush when Officer Thompson comes in by himself and has a seat at one of the booths.

I'm a little annoyed, if I'm being honest. He's by himself and taking up a four-top? Inconsiderate ass. Though, to be sure, he's always been that way. Which still doesn't excuse him. Not by a long shot.

I grab the coffee and a cup before heading his way, setting the cup down and filling it. "How are you, Officer?"

He grunts. "Patty melt with fries and onion rings. And a water."

I raise an eyebrow. "I'm fine, Willa. Thanks for asking. And how are you?"

He blinks up at me.

I smile back at him. "Conversation in polite society. You remember how that goes?"

He blinks again.

"Guess that's a no. Got it!" I say breezily, then turn away.

Mom's eyes are wide as I walk behind the counter to call the order out to Dad and hang the ticket on the wheel. "Willa Dean Dash!" she whisper-hisses.

"What?" I ask.

"Since when do you talk like that to, well, to *anyone*, let alone one of our men in uniform?"

I open my mouth to object, but close it. She's right. "Huh. Guess that's new, isn't it?" I fill a glass with ice and water for Thompson, then toast Mom with it.

I keep moving, trying not to drop anything or trip over my own two feet. Not ten minutes later, Officer Thompson's food is ready. I grab it and begin walking it to the booth, then slow. Another man with slicked-back hair has joined him. He looks vaguely familiar, but I can't place him. He smiles as I get close, but it's more of a leer as he sweeps his eyes up and down my body.

Ew.

"Patty melt with fries," I announce as I set the plate down, "and a side of onion rings," and place the other down.

"And who is this pretty little thing?" Creepy Man drawls.

"Excuse me?"

"You'll have to forgive him." Officer Thompson's gaze never leaves his table mate. "He doesn't seem to have manners."

The creep doesn't appear to be bothered by Thompson in the slightest. He slithers out of the booth, forcing me to step back and nearly fall into the table behind me, as he leers again. "Maybe I'll see you around." His breath is stale as he winks at me.

I try not to gag.

"Box this up." Officer Thompson gestures at his plate as the other guy leaves.

I stare at the cop and remind myself that he's a customer. Nah, screw it. "The word you're looking for is 'please'."

He rolls his eyes. "Please."

I grab the plates and pivot away, furious and also entirely freaked out. Mom eyes me as I return and grab a to-go box.

"Something wrong with the food?"

Then I remember the booth is the only one hidden from where Mom works at the counter, and I have to wonder if he chose that spot on purpose.

I shake myself. I've spent too much time around Reid: I'm finding suspicious behavior lurking behind every corner. And Thompson may be an asshole, but he's an asshole who's a police officer.

Naturally, he leaves no tip.

The next few hours fly by, and soon enough, I'm helping Dad clean the kitchen and get a few things prepped for tomorrow. Before long, he shoos me away. "I've got other people who work here, you know," he chides.

"Yeah, but how many of them can slice a tomato that pretty?" I joke, untying my apron and giving him a kiss on his fleshy cheek. He smells of Old Spice and the grill, a scent that is perfectly Dad in the best kind of way. "Love you, Dad."

He squeezes me to his side. "Love you too, Pumpkin. Now get out of here."

I give Mom a hug as well, reveling in her strong embrace. The woman is a championship hug-giver, and I make sure to get at least one per shift.

At home, I find Reid in the backyard like always, Midnight frolicking around him. The kitten's cast is entirely off, thanks to

Matty's care. She darts up to me, batting at my shoelaces as I close the distance to Hottie Boombalottie playing guitar in the Adirondack chair.

"Hey, you." I sink into his lap as he sets the guitar aside.

He nuzzles my neck. "You don't smell nearly as much like onion rings as you normally do."

I laugh. "Because I waitressed today."

He pulls away. "Did anyone get hurt?"

"Meanie," I giggle, attempting to swat at him.

He captures my hand with his and brings it to his lips, kissing it instead.

I will not fall for him. I will not fall for him goes through my head. But who am I kidding? I fell for the guy pretty much right after I almost literally fell for him.

Then I sniff. "Wait a minute."

He raises his eyebrows and grins. "I was wondering when you'd smell that."

I look around. "Since when did your rental house come with a smoker?"

"Since I had Bob from the hardware store deliver and assemble it for me this morning," comes the smug answer.

"And what, pray tell, is in there?"

"Oh, come on now. You can't use your highly-trained sniffer to figure that out?"

I purse my lips. "Fine." Then I stand up, pick Midnight up for a cuddle, and take a few steps toward the smoker on the back porch.

"No cheating!" Reid calls.

"Ribs," I announce, turning to him triumphantly.

"That's my girl," he says with a grin. He wraps an arm around me and leads me to the grill, but I'm still trying to process what just came out of his mouth.

That's my girl?

Since when?

And why did my stupid heart soar at the phrase?

He opens the smoker for my inspection. "It'll be ready soon. Plenty of time for you to take a shower."

I smile up at him and take the kiss he plants on my temple. This whole scene feels oddly…domestic.

Then again, what have we been doing the past few weeks but playing house?

I have got to get better about this.

I slide out from beneath his arm. "Sounds good." I ignore the confused look on his face as I head inside for a shower, but deposit Midnight on the ground before going in. At least one female can give him love without expecting anything in return.

Freshly showered, I go back outside to find that Reid has put together a picnic. I join him at the table, grinning and forcing myself out of the sullen mood I'd been in. "This looks wonderful."

He sets a beer down in front of me with a flourish. It's a classic set-up: pork ribs dripping with what I assume is home-made sauce, potato salad, thick slices of white bread, and baked beans.

"Not gonna lie, I hope these are good," he says. "It's been a while since I've smoked anything, and I didn't have as long to do it as I'd like."

I take a bite. "They're delicious."

He preens.

"I could have done better, obviously," I tease him, "but not bad for a guy from Florida."

We eat and talk, studiously avoiding any topic that might lead to a deeper discussion on my part.

"That was delicious." I lick the sauce from my fingers, delighting in the way his eyes darken as they watch.

"You should be careful with the way you're using that tongue, Willa," he warns.

I grin. "Come on. Let's clean all this up and we'll see what else I have to lick."

Later, after a round of sex in which he had me screaming his name so many times I lost count, I remember the encounter with Thompson and the creep at the diner.

"You okay?" Reid asks, his eyes searching mine.

I shift in his arms. "Yeah. Just remembering something at work today."

"Wanna talk about it?"

"Nah." He has to work with Thompson, and I don't want to make things awkward between the two of them. I reach down to grab his dick. "I have a better idea."

CHAPTER 24

REID

T'S BEEN ALMOST a week since the last rabbit's foot on my doorknob. Normally, this is exactly when I'd find something else. Maybe a head this time, or a rabbit's foot that isn't one from a store. I was with these guys enough to know their tactics.

The thing is, I find nothing. No strangers lurking at the diner, no one looking out of place during my patrols, and no more squatters. They've gone dark, and if the idea was to send me into a nervous tailspin of anxiety, wondering if they were going to target me or Willa next, then they've succeeded.

"You in there, Officer Reid?" Tom's hand waves in front of my face as he and Jerry watch me with open curiosity.

I snap back to attention. "Sorry. What?"

"We were just wondering if you and Willa planned on five kids or ten," Jerry jokes.

"Boys, you leave him alone," Barbara admonishes as she refills my coffee.

I give her a nod of thanks and scowl at the old-timers.

Tom looks appraisingly at me. "You gonna let her mom fight your battles now, too?"

"Come on, boys," I say, "we all know that Willa's gonna leave us all in the dust one day."

Willa's head snaps up from the grill, as though she heard me. She probably did. She's back there making another one of my ridiculous orders—today is the Hashbrown Heaven Special, but of course I don't want the onions, I want scallions. And I don't want the actual hash that this one comes with; I want sausage.

She'd been put out, glaring at me from the window while I smiled like a happy schoolboy right back at her.

I absolutely love riling her up. That might be the best part of my day.

Actually, no. Making Willa come is the best part of my day.

Maybe it's making her smile.

Good lord, what is happening to me? The only time I even remotely relax these days is when I'm with her, threat of the Bunnies be damned.

She has a chokehold on me. To the point where it's starting to dawn on me that I might be falling for her. There's no other way to explain the constant pressure in my chest.

Unless it's heartburn.

But no amount of Tums is curing it, so I'm pretty sure I'm falling for her. Which is absurd, because I'm going back to Miami. Right?

I'm...not so sure anymore.

The click of a shutter going off beside me brings me back to reality once more, and I turn to find JJ inspecting his camera screen in the wake of taking a photo.

"Hand it over," I state.

He looks up at me, startled. "I've got every right—"

I slide off the stool and use every bit of my bulk against his scrawny stature. "I said, hand it over."

His eyes wide, he hands the expensive camera to me.

I look at the screen. Sure enough, it's another photo of me. I delete it, then hand the camera back at him.

He stares at the camera in shock. "Hey! You can't do that," he protests.

"I can, and I did," I say, my voice low. I know I sound like an asshole—and, truthfully, I'm being one—but Willa's safety is at risk. So I continue. "If you take one more picture of me without my consent, or if you print anything about me in your paper, I will make your life uncomfortable. Do you understand me?"

He blinks and takes a step back. "It's just—"

I should feel bad. He's doing his job. But again: Willa. And for her, there's no compromise. "No. There is no 'just' about this. There is a 'yes, I understand' answer, and it is the only answer."

He nods. "Okay."

I step forward, crowding him and making his back bow a little. "I didn't hear you."

He licks his lips nervously. "I said, okay, I won't take any more pictures of you."

I straighten and smile, clapping him on the back far harder than is necessary. "Wonderful! Have a seat. Get some lunch. I'll buy."

He pales. "I'll, uh, pass."

I grin maniacally at him. "You sure?"

He nods and backs up. "Yeah. Thanks, ah, thanks anyway."

I watch with no small amount of pleasure as he skitters away.

"Was that really necessary?" Barbara asks, setting my order in front of me as I slide back onto my stool.

I look at my lunch, then back up to Barbara, her daughter and husband working the grill like a well-oiled machine behind her. "Yes," I say simply.

I don't bother fighting the instinct a few hours later to drive Willa home after her shift. She looks up in surprise when I pull up in the squad car. "Reid?"

I lean over and open the passenger door. "Get in. I'll take you home."

She waves her hand at her car. "I drove. And isn't it against the law to ride in a cop car?"

"We'll figure your car out later. And if you want me to cuff you, I'd be happy to do so." I wiggle my eyebrows suggestively.

She laughs as she gets in the car. "You're insane."

I breathe a little easier with her safely beside me.

I *don't* breathe easier as she climbs out at her house and winks at me, pulling her hair down from her ponytail and swaying her hips as she walks away from the car.

Fuck. Me.

I put the car in park and radio Betty. "Taking a break, Betty. Give me twenty?"

"You got it, big guy," comes the response.

I kill the engine and hustle after Willa. I have a diner cook to give an orgasm to.

I growl in frustration when I see she's left the door not just unlocked, but wide open.

"Willa, dammit," I call.

Then she appears in my view, utterly naked and grinning wickedly at me. "I'm sorry, Officer. Did I do something wrong?"

Well, hello there. I close and lock the door, then unbuckle my utility belt before stalking to her. "You naughty girl. I think you might have to pay for that."

She squeals and makes to turn away, but I grab her by the wrist. I turn it just enough to catch her off-guard and pull her back flush against my front. "I didn't get enough to eat during lunch," I murmur against her neck.

She squirms against me. "I need a shower."

I release her and point to the bed. "Get your pretty ass on that bed and give me your pussy."

Her eyes flare, but she hesitates.

I reach down and pull her into a bridal carry before she can process what I've just done, then lay her on the bed. I yank her legs to bring her ass to the edge, then kneel before her.

"Reid, seriously," she protests.

"Look at me."

She does, a faint blush appearing on those beautiful cheeks.

"Whose pussy is this?"

Her blush deepens. "Yours."

"And if I want to eat it, I get to eat it. Whenever I want."

She swallows. "Okay."

I narrow my eyes and press my fingers into her thighs. "Okay, *what?*"

"Okay, Officer MacKinnon."

"Don't you dare look away from me, Willa. Watch me make you come."

And once I've made her scream my name, I go back on shift.

CHAPTER 25

WILLA

I WAKE UP to birds chirping outside, the morning sun slanting through the gauzy curtains and highlighting Reid's sleeping form beside me. He's so beautiful lying there. No worries to crease his brow, nothing to make him scowl thoughtfully as he looks at me or the rest of the world around him. He inhales deeply, and the movement brings my attention to the shiny pink wound on his shoulder.

I know it wasn't a routine traffic stop. I know he's hiding something from me. Maybe if he were mine, I'd have more to say about it. But I don't get all his secrets. There's always a part of him that stays hidden, something in the background that keeps him from opening up entirely to me.

None of it keeps me from loving him.

I know it's foolish. I know it's going to hurt like hell when he leaves, but it'd be even more foolish to let this experience pass me by.

I know I'm sheltered. God knows that it's been proven time and time again. But I'm okay with that. It's okay that my first real taste of the world was getting yelled at on a reality cooking show that scarred me so badly I never went back. I've forgiven myself for my reaction, but it seems I need to make my parents understand that still.

Reid takes another deep inhale and rolls over, his eyes fluttering open as he smiles at me.

My heart melts. Yeah, I'm positive I'm in love with him. The words bubble up to my throat and nearly pop out of my mouth, but I manage to keep them swallowed.

"Good morning, gorgeous." His voice is thick with sleep.

"Hi," I whisper.

"How long have you been awake and staring at me?"

I shrug. "Not long."

He grins and pulls me to him for a kiss. It's sweet and gentle, and I sigh happily into it. Reid's always like this in the mornings: light and unencumbered by whatever dark thoughts consume him throughout the rest of the day. It lasts for all of five minutes, and I cherish every second of it.

His beard rasps across my skin as we kiss, and he hums contentedly. When our make-out session is complete, we haul ourselves out of bed and cook breakfast together. It's Sunday, and yoga's in a couple of hours, so we prepare a simple feast of eggs over easy, layered on top of avocado, tomato, and buttery sourdough bread.

After that, we wash up and take quick showers. We're heading to the car for yoga when Reid's phone dings. He looks at it, then pales.

"What happened?"

"It's Jack. He's in the hospital."

We head straight there. Reid puts Betty on speaker as he speeds to the hospital.

"He's been shot at close range. He's in surgery already."

Reid curses, flying through an intersection after barely braking. "We'll be there soon."

Grabbing onto the handle above the window, I risk a glance at him. He looks like a ghost, his knuckles bleached white from the grip he has on the steering wheel.

"It's going to be okay, Reid," I whisper.

He releases a strangled sound. "You don't know that."

Nothing more is said until we get to the hospital, when I tell him to pull into the ER and offer to park the truck.

For once, he takes me up on the offer, throwing the engine into park and sprinting out, the door wide open in his wake.

My heart hurts for him as I send a plea to the universe. *Please let Chief be okay.*

I park the truck and book it to the ER, where the desk nurse tells me what floor to head up to. By the time I make it there, Reid is already giving Officer Thompson nothing short of an interrogation, judging by the purple tinge to the man's face.

"Well?" Reid prompts.

Thompson scowls. "I told you, I'm here to get a statement from Chief when he wakes up."

It's clear that Reid is as much of a fan of the other cop as the rest of us. He opens his mouth to speak, but seems to think better of it.

"Reid," I say quietly, hoping to distract him and defuse the situation. "Come sit."

With a final, scathing look at his fellow officer, Reid joins me in the row of pea-green chairs against the wall. The air is thick with tension as he sits beside me and pulls his phone out, his fingers flying over the keys.

"I need to let my parents know what's happening," he mutters. When his phone rings a moment later with 'Dad' flashing across the screen, he stands and answers it as he walks away. "Yeah, I haven't heard anything yet," he says.

Across the room, Thompson takes a seat.

Two interminable hours later, the doctor emerges from surgery to announce everything went well and that Chief will be okay. Officer Thompson stands, ostensibly ready to head back to get Chief's statement, when Reid shoots him a look.

"He's pretty out of it," the doctor says, casting wary glances at the men. "But one of you can go see him for now."

Reid doesn't hesitate. "I'm his nephew."

It's another thirty minutes before Reid returns, but when he does, his face is thunderous. I've never seen him so angry, and it's hard not to wilt under his gaze. With a blink, the anger fades as he regards me, and he holds his hand out. When I take it, the grip is soft and reassuring.

"How is he?" I ask, stepping closer.

He shakes his head.

"Do you want to stay?"

With another shake, he leads me out. I follow him to the truck and give him his keys, and we get in. He starts the engine and turns toward the interstate, heading east.

"Where are we going?"

"Is it okay if I say I don't know?"

I bite my lower lip. "Sure." Once we're on the highway, I try again. "Did Chief Mac say what happened?"

He opens his mouth to speak, but closes it, running a hand through his hair and blowing out an agitated breath.

I reach over to touch his arm. "You can talk to me, you know."

He flinches, and my hand hovers in the air as he shakes his head. "I can't," he says, his voice steely. "You can't help. No one can."

The change in him isn't huge, but I've learned to read his subtleties: The way he tenses at any hint of sharing what bothers him. The tic of his jaw. The way his grip on the steering wheel bleaches his knuckles. I scoff. "Of course no one can help, Reid— you won't tell anyone what's going on. Before now, I probably wouldn't have said anything. Stayed quiet and let it be. But Chief Mac got *shot* and you can't even tell me what happened?"

"Willa—"

"I'm not finished," I interrupt him, surprised at myself but embracing it all the same. "You can keep it all bottled up. That's your right. But I'm tired of your secrets, Reid. I know you have them. *Everyone* knows you have them. And I guess I thought by now that you'd at least share a little bit with me. Was I wrong?"

He flips the blinker and takes the next exit, one that leads to a beach. "You're right."

"I know I'm right. But what are you going to do about it?"

He glances at me, then reaches a hand across the console to cover mine, his palm warm and reassuring. "Give me a chance to explain?"

I hesitate. *Be brave.* "Will you finally tell me what's been going on?" I pause. "Including the gunshot wound?"

Pulling into a public lot next to the beach, he turns off the ignition. "Yes. I'll tell you everything."

"And you better make it good, Reid MacKinnon. I'm tired of being in the dark."

His shoulders drop with relief and he shoots me an affectionate glance. "Look at you, standing up for yourself," he teases, the moment lightening.

I snort softly. "Come on."

We make our way to the beach, pulling off our shoes and leaving them just off the entrance next to several other pairs. We've walked a good half mile before he speaks, the ocean lapping at our feet and keeping us cool in the early September heat. He takes a deep breath and lets it out. "I lied to you."

My heart sinks with his revelation. There's a difference in suspecting something versus knowing it outright, and it hurts. Still, I stay silent and wait on him to continue.

"I told you I was shot during a routine traffic stop, but that's not true." His knuckles graze mine. "I spent the last three years working undercover to infiltrate a drug organization called the Bunnies."

I gawk at him, puzzled. "The...*Bunnies*? You're kidding, right?"

His face is a mask of grim determination. "No. They sound harmless, but they most definitely aren't. Not even close. I was doing pretty well, rising through the ranks and gathering evidence as I went. But it all went sideways a couple of months ago. Someone got suspicious. When they called me on it, I had no choice." He looks out to the water. "I did what I had to do, but it resulted in three people dead. One of whom was the boss's son."

I suck air in, trying to wrap my head around the story. It sounds like the plot of a movie. And killing the mob boss's son? "Oh, no."

He huffs out a laugh. "Yeah. Oh no. I immediately went underground. Got treated for the gunshot, and my chief told me to lay low. At the same time, Uncle Jack reached out about needing some help in Lucky. It seemed like a win-win. My chief agreed, so after about a month, when we knew the heat had lifted a little, I came here."

"How did anyone think you working as a small-town cop was a good way to lie low?" I ask, incredulous.

"Such a good question, Willa." He shakes his head. "And honestly? I don't know. None of us thought they were operating this far away from Miami."

Dread snakes across my body. "Are they…here? In Lucky?

"Uncle Jack was shot by the Bunnies," he says flatly.

My hand flies to my mouth. "Oh my God."

"It's so much worse than that." His voice breaks. "They know where I live. They've left two rabbit feet on my fucking doorknob in warning. And when I talked to Jack, he said the man tossed a rabbit's foot at him before shooting him. If he hadn't moved the way he did—" He cuts off.

"Hey." I stop, halting his stride and pulling him to me. The water laps at our feet and I tighten my arms around him. "It's okay. We'll figure this out. We'll get through it."

He pulls away and stares at me.

"What?"

"You said *we*. That *we* would get through this."

I blink, confused. "Well, yeah. Of course. What else would I say?"

He looks at the ocean for a beat, then focuses back on me. "I don't deserve this."

"Deserve what? Kindness?" I almost say 'love,' but swallow it at the last moment.

"You, Willa," he murmurs. "I don't deserve *you*."

"Why not? I'm not special."

He tucks a strand of hair behind my ear, then cups my face in his hands, his eyes soft and adoring. "Sweetheart, you are absolutely special. You are the best of everything in this world, beautiful and wondrous. But me? I am nothing but trouble for the people I love. Clearly."

My heart hitches at the word. The word I almost said but kept inside. The word that I've not dared to hope would come out of his mouth. The word that I was eventually going to lose him over. And now? What happens? Does he even mean what I think he means? "Reid." It sounds more like a question than anything.

He squeezes his eyes shut. "I just...said that out loud, didn't I?"

I almost laugh, still not quite sure what to do here. My heart is galloping. "You did. But, Reid?"

He peeks an eye open and looks down at me, one of his stupid dimples popping as he gives me a bashful look. "Yeah?"

I take a deep breath and exhale. No time like the present to keep taking those steps to be brave, I suppose. "I love you, too."

A thousand different emotions play over his face, but the one that finally lands is something between relief and disbelief. He picks me up and swirls me around the low tide, and I squeal as he grips me tight.

After he sets me down, he cups my face once more. "Willa Dean Dash, you are everything." When he kisses me, it's tender and searching, soft and sweet, and as the surf slowly buries our feet in the sand and water, all I can think is how in love with this man I am.

Underneath it all, though, I'm scared. Scared of this new chapter, but also scared of what he's told me. All I can do is hold on to the man I love. It'll all work out.

Somehow.

CHAPTER 26

REID

"**F**UCK, REID, *YES!*"

Willa's thighs squeeze my head as she bucks and writhes, lost to the orgasm.

I give her no time to recover, rolling on a condom and rising to thrust into her as I stand on the ground, her legs thrown up against me. "Don't stop coming, gorgeous."

Her eyes widen as her pussy clenches around my cock, a pink blush blooming on her body. I piston into her, desperate to keep her going as she whimpers and mews.

I woke up to her kissing her way to my cock, but fuck if I was going to come before she did. So I flipped us, yanked her to the edge of the mattress, and buried my face in her pussy.

I want this forever. I don't know how to make that happen.

My own release builds quickly, not helped by the vision of this beautiful woman before me, her dark hair tousled by sleep, her blue eyes hazy with lust and pleasure, her tits bouncing with every thrust into her, and those lips, moaning and telling me things that make me believe this could last forever.

Her walls pulse hard around my cock, and I yell as I come inside her, nearly blacking out in the wake of it.

She laughs as I pull out and stumble to the bathroom to get rid of the condom. She's sitting upright when I return, her eyes bright and full of mischief. "Is that gonna happen every morning I try to give you a blowjob? Because if so, sign me up."

"You're trouble," I chide, shaking my head.

Sliding off the bed and closing the distance between us, she wraps her arms around me and kisses my chest. "But I'm the best kind, right?"

I smack her ass. "Definitely. Come on—I'll start the shower."

THERE ARE TWO WORDS TO DESCRIBE ME: POSSESSED and obsessed.

Possessed with an unwavering need to find the asshole who shot my uncle.

Obsessed with the way Willa told me she loved me. Not just yesterday, but this morning, too, as she got out of my truck in front of the diner.

Even though I didn't *quite* say it back. But I do. Love her, that is. It's just…what happens now? I've got four weeks left in this town.

How am I supposed to do this?

My hands itch to pick up the phone and call Dad, to hear him give me shit and tell me I know exactly what to do. But I don't. Because what I really should be focused on is who shot my uncle. Finding that asshole and putting him behind bars. Or in the ground if he's dumb enough to try anything.

Honestly, I wish he would.

"Mind if I use Chief's office?" I ask Betty, tilting my head toward the only place in the station with a door. "I need to make a call."

She peers up at me. "You trying to find who did this to our chief?"

"Obviously," I deadpan.

She sniffs. "Fine. But don't get comfortable in there—Chief will be back before you know it."

"I'm counting on it."

In the office, I close the door and take a deep breath. I need to be calm when I tell Chief Muñoz what happened yesterday. After a moment, I punch his number.

"MacKinnon."

"They shot my uncle." My voice shakes, all pretense of calm wiped away as soon as I open my mouth. "They fucking shot my uncle, Chief."

"Chief MacKinnon?"

"The very same."

Muñoz swears. "The DA is back on track. We grabbed another one of their grunts and he's rolling on them for a deal."

I pinch the bridge of my nose. "That's good, but how's that helping me find who did this?"

He sighs. "You know the routine, MacKinnon. Work the case. Follow the evidence. And for fuck's sake, lay low."

"That ship has sailed, Chief." I relay the rabbit feet and my security cameras giving me nothing.

He swears again. "What the hell have you been doing up there? What part of 'lie low' did you not understand? It was a mistake allowing you to patrol."

"Probably," I admit, recalling Willa's question yesterday. "Definitely, in fact. But what's done is done." I don't bother mentioning that my picture is probably all over at least twenty different tourists' social media pages.

Besides, I'm certain—well, fairly certain—that it wasn't those pages that outed me. It was JJ. "I still don't know how they picked up that I was up here, Chief. To be honest, it's all a little fishy."

He snorts. "You think? Just do what I said: Work the case."

"Yes, sir."

We finish the call, and shame twists in my gut. If I'd been more careful—hell, if I hadn't come to this town at all—my uncle wouldn't be lying in a hospital room recovering from a gunshot wound absolutely intended to kill him. But then I wouldn't have met Willa. I groan, frustrated. This whole thing is shit. I can't play the *what-if* game, or I'll drive myself crazy. Yanking the door so hard it slams against the wall, I stalk to Betty's desk. She looks up from her romance novel, an eyebrow raised.

"Was that really necessary?"

"You look way too much like your mother when you do that," I retort.

She blanches. "A helpful hint, Reid: Don't ever tell a woman she's just like her mother."

I chuckle. "Fair enough. I need your help—but quietly. Can you get me the logs of every single call that's come into the station over the past two months?"

"That's a decent number of calls, Officer MacKinnon," she says, her mouth tipped up in a satisfied smile. "You got an idea brewing?"

"I might."

A few hours later, I have a headache from reviewing all the data. But I also have a hunch.

CHAPTER 27

WILLA

R EID DIDN'T STAY over last night. Except for our conversation on the beach and a few glorious hours yesterday morning, Reid's spent all his available time in the two days since Chief Mac got shot looking for who did it.

I don't blame him, but I miss him all the same.

I finish my shift at the diner on Tuesday and head for my usual shower, then go to Agatha's for tea. I saw Reid's truck outside, but he wasn't in the backyard, and when I looked at his house, he wasn't in there waving at me like he's been before.

Admittedly, it stings. Is this what happens after I tell someone I love them?

Agatha meets me at her screen door, gesturing to the porch and telling me to have a seat. I settle into the porch swing and wait, knowing she won't let me help her because she never does.

When Agatha comes out, she's trailed by none other than Reid, who looks breathtaking in a simple pair of faded jeans and a heather gray T-shirt. The shirt is tight around his biceps, and I swear they flex as I look at them, as if Reid knows that's where my attention goes and does it on purpose. When I met his eyes, he's smiling mischievously, so maybe he did notice.

"Hi, Willa." His voice is smooth, silky.

"Hi, Reid."

Agatha sets the tray of tea and glasses on the table, then pours some for all of us. She tops the drinks with big rounds of lemon, and the whole effect is pretty as a picture.

"Cheers," she says, easing into her seat as Reid joins me on the swing.

We clink our glasses together and take a sip, and I close my eyes at the taste, strong and tart with a hint of mint. It's hard to top a breezy afternoon on a porch swing with a perfect glass of iced tea.

"I suppose you're both wondering why I've called you here," Agatha begins.

I wasn't, actually, but I nod and smile alongside Reid.

"Is everything okay?" he asks.

She waves him off. "Of course. I just figured it's my duty as your landlord and neighbor to get the—what do the kids say?— the 'hot goss' from the two of you. Are you together or what?"

I nearly choke on the tea, and Reid slaps my back and looks at me quizzically. I narrow my gaze at him as I recover, then smile sweetly at him. "Reid?"

His eyes widen. "Me?" I smirk, and he turns to Agatha. "Well, um," he begins. "I guess we're, ah, seeing each other?" He looks at me helplessly.

Heck, *I* want to know what's going on with us, too, so I wait for him to finish.

Clearing his throat, he continues, "And, well…that's it. We're seeing each other."

Agatha adjusts her glasses to peer at him, then swings her gaze to me. "And are you moving to Miami with him, dear? Finally going to make good on your mother's dreams for you and cook in a Michelin-starred restaurant? Lord knows it's all she talks about."

My heart squeezes. Mom's been more and more vocal about it

since Reid got here, and it…hurts. I know she means well. I look at Agatha, my feet barely touching the ground, as Reid swings us on the porch swing. "Honestly, Agatha?"

She nods seriously, not even a hint of wanting the 'hot goss.' I think she simply cares.

I give her the truth. "No."

Beside me, Reid stiffens almost imperceptibly.

I keep going. "Lucky is my home. It's always been my home, and I've been, well, *lucky* enough to feel like this is my forever home since I can remember the idea even occurring to me. Not everyone feels like they belong in the town where they were born, but I do. I'm staying here. It might mean that I have to open my own place eventually, but for now, I'm happy exactly where I am."

Agatha smacks her hands on her lap decidedly, as though she was waiting for me to make this very declaration, then turns her impressive attention to Reid. "Your turn, Reid."

"Ma'am?" He nearly croaks the word.

"Are you going back to Miami or staying here?"

My heart sinks at the question, because I already know the answer. Reid, ever-observant man that he is, notices. He puts his warm palm on top of my free hand where it lies on the white slats of the swing. "I'm, ah, not yet sure. I have a lot going on—"

Agatha quite literally *pshaws* him, which I have never seen in real life, and can confirm that it is as satisfying as I thought it might be.

Reid gawks. "Excuse me?"

She does it again. "You heard me. Pshaw. Pa-*shaw*."

He blinks at her. "Are you— choking?"

I stifle a hysterical giggle, not sure if I should be laughing or coming to Reid's rescue, but decide it's far better to listen.

Agatha harrumphs. "You listen to me, Reid MacKinnon. Your uncle is laying in the hospital over there, shot by who knows what kind of terrible person, and those kinds of things should bring a person clarity."

"Erm, okay…" Reid drawls.

"So, get clear!" She throws up her hands. "I swear, young people are as stupid as the day is long."

I cough out a laugh.

"I'm…sorry?" Reid says.

She stands and points at us. "You should be. I'm done with you two." She gestures in frustration and goes inside.

Reid and I look at each other. "Do you know—?" he starts.

But the screen door squeaks open and Agatha's head pokes out. "And clean this up. I don't want ants." Her head disappears, and the door bounces shut behind her.

Reid chuckles and shakes his head. "This is the part about living in small towns that I didn't believe was actually true."

"Oh, it's very true." I stand and start cleaning up the glasses, tidying everything to take back inside Agatha's kitchen.

"You don't have to do that, you know."

I glance up at him. "Do what?"

"Clean up."

I scoff. "What did she say? Pa-*shaw*?"

He quirks a grin. "She did."

"Then I'm saying that same thing to you. Just—wait here? Probably best only one of us goes in there in case she decides to launch another offensive."

He opens the door for me and waits as requested. I put everything away and return to the porch.

"Come on, I'll walk you home," he says.

My chest squeezes at the phrasing. Not *can I come in* or *let's watch some bad television and I'll rub your feet,* but *I'll walk you home.* All I can do is nod, swallowing the thickness in my throat and unable to speak.

But when we get to the door, he follows me inside and shuts the door behind him, locking it. He opens his arms and I sink into them, wanting the world to stop for just a little while. Wanting simply to feel safe and wanted in Reid's arms. Not to worry about what happens next, or how I'm supposed to love a man like Reid, who keeps secrets so habitually that even now, it feels like I barely know anything about him.

"I know this isn't forever, Reid. I get it," I finally manage to say, my voice muffled against his shirt.

"Willa," he sighs.

"But it's hard. So freaking hard," I sniff, unwilling to cry. I will not cry.

Yeah, I'm gonna cry.

"I love you, and you're going to break my heart," I choke out.

"Fuck, Willa, you're breaking *my* heart," he says softly, tipping my chin up and kissing me gently.

He peels my clothes off right there in the kitchen, and when he scoops me into his arms to walk me to the bedroom, I try hard not to wonder how many more times I'll get this. Get him.

We make love slowly, tenderly, as though it might be the last time. When I come, I manage to hold back the tears until his head is buried in the crook of my neck.

Later, we have a simple dinner of pasta with red sauce and garlic bread. We're lounging on the couch with Midnight, her little body splayed between us, the fuzz on her stomach sticking straight up and just begging for pets, when I say, "You have to take her with you." I barely get the words out, and they're so soft I'm almost surprised he heard them.

"Tonight? I thought I'd stay with you, if that's okay."

"I meant when you leave. When—when you go back to Miami."

He blanches.

And suddenly, I can't do this anymore. I stand. "I think you should go." I nod, as if I'm agreeing with myself. This is me, standing up for myself. *Go, me!*

Except, why does it feel so bad?

Reid looks up at me, silent, his forest-green eyes searching my face. Dimly, I wonder if he's ever been trained to read emotions. Not that mine are any secret. I'm a mess.

"I'll see you tomorrow. Come by the diner, and I'll make you a burger. No sesame seeds." My voice pitches higher as I speak, and I turn away, tears already streaming down my cheeks. I fight hard to keep from collapsing in on myself, but there's no stopping the way my shoulders shake with silent sobs.

I don't hear anything at first, but after a moment, there's the telltale sound of him rising from the couch and moving toward the kitchen.

I simply…can't.

Can't move. Can't breathe. It takes everything I have to hold myself upright.

"I'll get Midnight in the morning," he says. And it's the wobble in his voice, and the way he knocks on the glass window as he leaves, reminding me to turn the lock, that does it.

I run to the kitchen, slamming against the door. But instead of opening it and yelling for him to come back, that I'm sorry and I didn't mean it and I want whatever we have for as long as we can have it, I choke out a sob and lock it.

Then I slide to the floor and cry.

REID

TO SAY I slept like shit would be the direst understatement of understatements.

Come to think of it, I'm not sure I slept at all.

I splash water on my face, chug a bottle of water, and throw on my running clothes. After a cursory check of the security feeds and viewing a playback to be certain no one came around either of our houses last night, I step outside and break into a dead sprint. Anything not to think about the words that Willa said.

I wanted her to learn to stand up for herself, sure. But to do it with me was a curve ball I didn't see coming.

My chest aches. I gulp in air and take a turn on the sidewalk like I'm some kind of Formula 1 racer. With every pound of my shoes on the pavement, all I can think about is her. *I think you should leave.*

What's worse is that I planned to tell her I loved her.

I shake my head and push harder.

No, I wasn't. I'm a fucking coward, and I wasn't going to tell her shit.

How does a big-city guy like me waltz into this town and get schooled by a tiny little diner cook?

Because you're an ignorant, egotistical asshole, that's how.

I head to visit Uncle Jack after I get cleaned up and put on my uniform, radioing Betty on my way over to tell her what I'm doing.

Jack is sitting up and finishing something that is supposed to be breakfast, but based on the grimace he wears as he stares at it glumly, I don't expect he's enjoying it too much. "Chief."

His expression morphs as he looks up to grin at me. "Good to see you, son. Come on in and distract me from this." He pushes the tray to the side and folds his hands in his lap.

No point in beating around the bush. "I need to talk to you about the case."

He nods. "I figured."

I look around, then lean forward and lower my voice. "Is anyone supposed to be coming by soon? A doctor? Ox? Thompson?"

Jack narrows his eyes. "I know that trick, Reid. Hell, I may have even taught it to you. Shut that door and tell me what Thompson did."

Raising my eyebrows, I do as he says and pull a chair close to him. I'm not interested in my hunch being broadcast to the world. "First, answer me something. I know I asked already, but I'm going to ask again. Did you get any kind of look at the guy who shot you?"

His face hardens with frustration. "No. Someone knocked at my door, and I went to answer it. I open the door, and something gets tossed at my chest. I bend down to catch it, reflexes and all that, and the next thing I know, a pair of black boots and pants are in my line of vision. Then I hear a pop, and I'm shot." He shakes his head. "I've gone over it a million ways. Whoever it was, they knew when to strike, and they had a clean shot. If I'd not bent down to grab that stupid rabbit foot…"

My jaw clenches so hard I might crack a tooth. "I know. That's their signature. They left two on my front door in the weeks leading up to them shooting you." I sigh and rub a hand over my face. "I'm…Jesus, Jack. I'm so sorry. This is all my fault."

"No," he responds, his tone brooking no argument. "You listen to me, Reid, and listen well. This isn't your fault."

"They're after *me*."

"That may be, but you're not the one who shot me. So it's not your fault."

I shake my head, unconvinced. "Your word against mine, Chief."

He sighs. "Just as stubborn as your dad, you know that? You going to tell me your hunch?"

I scoot forward in answer. "I asked Betty to pull all the calls that came into the station over the past two months. Then, I asked her to pull one more month because I was having a hard time believing what I was seeing."

"What kind of reports?"

"Any time it was about a crime. Not the ones about lost pets and resetting the town clock—the real ones."

Chief smiles softly. "You look a seven-year-old in the face and tell them that their missing iguana isn't a problem for the cops to solve and watch their reaction. I promise you, son, those are *real*."

I roll my eyes and chuckle. "Yeah, yeah, small-town guy. I get it. Anyway, the pattern. Every time it was a call about something bad happening, Thompson wasn't on shift."

Jack stills. "What?"

I nod. "I can't quite believe that this means he's our guy, but I'm having a hard time wondering if he doesn't somehow have something to do with them." There's more I want to say, about the way his prejudices aren't doing the residents of this town any good and how cops like him make our jobs that much harder, but now isn't the time.

With a sigh, my uncle says, "He wants to be chief, Reid. You need to think very carefully before you go throwing accusations like this around."

"Believe me, I get it. I do. But something's off with him. Don't tell me you never see it."

He shrugs. "There's always an odd duck or two on every police force. Figured that was just the role he was playing."

My eyes bug out. "And you think it's okay that he wants to be chief?"

Jack huffs. "Focus on the facts in front of you, Reid. Tell me more."

With a deep breath, I detail everything I learned, and how some of it mimics a lot of the things that are signatures of the Bunnies. At the end, my uncle simply stares at me.

I hold my hands up. "It's just a hunch."

"You're telling me there may be mob activity in my town? Going on right under my nose, and I've never seen it?"

"The Bunnies aren't exactly the mob," I hedge, "and I still have a hard time seeing how Thompson's connected to them, but Jack, I don't see any other way around it. Nothing else makes sense, despite how small-brained the man is."

He flattens his mouth into a thin line. "You've given me a lot to think about, Reid."

I stand, understanding the dismissal.

"Wait a minute."

I pause.

"How's Willa?"

My chest fucking caves. And apparently my expression goes right along with it.

His voice softens. "What happened, son?"

I scrub my hand over my face. "It's...complicated."

"It can't be more complicated than this." He gestures at himself.

"That might not be true," I sigh. "But I'm not ready to talk about it."

He regards me, then finally says, "With that kind of reaction, I don't blame you. Get out of here, then. Go work my case, will you?"

I give him a salute and turn to leave. I'll do what he says and work the case, but I have to see Willa first. She needs to know how I really feel.

I need to say the damn words.

I've never said them to anyone besides my family. You'd think, for a guy who grew up with a pretty great example of what a loving relationship could look like, that I'd have had the occasion to say it before now. But I haven't. Maybe it's that the relation-ship was between a parent and step-parent; maybe it's fear that my job would be an automatic deterrent to someone. But either way, the words need to come out of my mouth. The beach was the closest I've ever gotten, and my stomach nearly came out of my throat because I was so nervous to see her reaction.

I don't even know if she's going to speak to me. I don't know if *I'd* let myself speak to me.

I'm out of the elevator and heading for the squad car when my phone dings.

It's a picture of a dead rabbit.

Followed by a picture of Dash In Diner.

My whole world drops out from beneath my feet, and I kick into a dead run.

The drive takes too long. I break more laws than I can count to get there, my foot shaking on the gas pedal. Five minutes is an eternity. My heart is in my throat. This can't be happening.

I leave the car two blocks away and cover the rest on foot. There's a Closed sign on the front door, *Due to plumbing issues.*

Willa didn't text me this morning. She didn't bring Midnight over, either. What if they've hurt her? Or worse?

I can't let myself think like that. I raise my hand to bang on the door and yell for whoever's inside, but stop myself, all my training finally kicking in.

Think.

I can't call for back-up, mainly because this entire mess is my fault and I don't need anyone else being hurt. But also because I half expect Betty would send out a bulletin alerting the entire town to come rescue the new cop, despite her help earlier.

I go around to the back, staying close to the perimeter and checking my surroundings as I move. Nothing is out of the ordinary. In fact, there's even a plumbing truck parked back here, but a quick glance tells me that the sign on the white truck is just one big removable sign. Adrenaline ratchets up.

It's definitely the Bunnies.

Using the dumpster as cover, I get as close as I can, and that's when I hear crying. I can't tell who it is, though, so I crouch down and get into a position where I can actually see inside.

Barbara, Dean, and Goldie are tied up in the kitchen. I can't see them very well, but I know it's them. A tall, lanky man stands above them, lazily pointing a gun in their direction while he speaks to someone on the phone. Another man who must spend all his downtime at the gym swivels his attention between Dean, whose feet I can see, and the women, both of whom are crying.

Where is Willa?

"Yeah, we've got 'em. He'll show up. We're positive." A pause. "He saw the photos. Idiot has his phone settings to show it as read." He chuckles.

I barely suppress a groan. I really *am* an idiot. The last few months of my life flash before my eyes, and I realize that very damn thing could have been how I ultimately got made and then shot.

A commotion at the front has everyone going quiet. I listen, then bite back a curse. *Jerry.* The lanky man gets off the phone while the beefy one takes off to see what the fuss is about.

Now's my chance.

CHAPTER 29

___

WILLA

TWO HOURS EARLIER

My pillow is wet with tears when I wake up. No wonder, really, considering I cried myself to sleep and started crying every time I awoke during the night—which was a lot.

Midnight blinks sleepily from her spot on the pillow beside me. I don't know when she got on the bed, but it's not in me to move her off. She probably misses Reid as much as I do.

I'd like nothing better than to stay here and wallow in my self-induced misery, but I need to get to work. Who knows? Maybe today will be the day I finally tell Mom that she's stuck with me for the foreseeable future, and to lay off me for good.

I get ready for work and feed Midnight, who I know is completely able to stay on her own. Besides, Reid hasn't come to get her, so that's that.

I always drive in front of the diner before parking in the back, and today's no different. What is different, though, is the sign on the door. I slow to peer at it. *Closed due to plumbing issues.*

That's odd.

I pull my foot off the brake and am about to pull around to the back when I notice a van down the street.

Maybe I'm being paranoid, but I should drive past it. It's probably a tourist in a really bad choice of vehicle, but enough time around Reid has finally had an effect, it seems.

I drive past the van, but it's empty. Still, I should be careful. Just in case.

Not that Reid will care.

Which, fine, that might be unfair, but you know what? A girl gets to be unfair sometimes. Sue me.

I park another block away, giving myself enough distance from the sketchy-looking van to make a run for it if things go south.

Seriously, how is no one on the street right now? I know it's early, but usually I could count on seeing at least one or two people.

I walk to the diner, then crouch as I near the corner and sneak to the back. I feel a little silly, especially when I see it's a plumbing van. I'm about to rise and call out through the diner's back door, but then I freeze, barely stifling a gasp.

Because the skinny creep from the booth with Officer Thompson is here, pointing a gun at my parents and sister, while another guy, super fit and super scary, ties them up.

Fear courses through me like lightning, and my legs shake as I watch with tears streaming down my face.

"Don't hurt them!" Dad says.

Without a word, the scary one backhands him, sending Dad jerking to the side.

Mom and Goldie scream, then Goldie sobs, "Please let us go, please let us go," over and over.

Fear turns to rage. Actual, legitimate rage, unlike anything I have ever known. I have never wished that I was some sort of superhero badass, but right now, I'd give anything for some of that power. A third man enters my line of sight, and I go rigid.

Officer Ted fucking Thompson.

"Goldie," he leers, "I really need you to shut your trap, sweetheart."

"Don't you talk to my daughter like that!" Mom yells as Dad tries to get up from where he's been shoved onto the floor.

A gunshot goes off.

I scream, but no one hears me because Goldie and Mom scream, too. Dad's face is white as a sheet, and I frantically scan all three from where I crouch. They all seem fine, but I can't be sure. My hands shake as I pull my phone out and clutch it.

Thompson stalks to the creep from the diner. "I told you we weren't killing anyone. What the hell was that?"

I've seen enough. I scramble away from my hiding spot and run toward the front. Part of me wants to call Reid, but what if he's in there and I can't see him? And if I call and his phone rings, what then?

I can't take that chance. I call Ox.

"Willa?"

"Officer Thompson and two others have Mom, Dad, and Goldie tied up at the diner. I think it's got something to do with Reid." It's remarkable how calm I sound, given the way the phone is shaking in my hands.

Ox curses. "Where's Reid?"

"I don't know. They might—" I can't say the words. *They might have him, too.*

The sounds of a car door shutting and engine starting come through the speaker. "Get away from there. I'm two minutes from you."

Yeah, that's not happening, but I at least stay near the front with my eyes and ears peeled. When Ox arrives, I hiss at him from my hiding spot and he frowns, approaching me and pulling his gun out.

"Get out of here, Willa!"

I shake my head. "No."

He sighs as he scans the area. "How many are back there?"

"Three, from what I can tell. At least two have guns." I hold back a sob. "I'm scared, Ox."

"I know. I need you to leave, Willa. This is dangerous." He doesn't bother waiting for me to answer, instead peeking around the corner of the building before pressing his body against the brick and taking off.

I know I should leave. Obviously. And seeing Ox only made me shake even more, but I'll be damned if I'm going anywhere. The old Willa might have listened to Ox, but the new one? No way. That's my family in there.

Tom's old jalopy of a car pulls up to the front, and he and Jerry get out, utterly ignoring my frantic attempts to wave them away. "Tom! Jerry!" I hiss. "Over here!"

But Jerry's on a mission, stalking to the door with his hands on his hips, peering at the sign like it's been written by aliens. After a moment, he huffs and twists away to yell at Tom, sputtering, "Says they're closed due to plumbing issues!"

"What?" Tom hobbles forward.

Jerry raises his voice. "I said, they're closed due to plumbing issues!" He curses when he finally spots me, pointing and yelling even louder. "Why didn't you call me? I'm the damn plumber!" He turns and bangs on the door. "Dean! Barbara! Open up!"

They're going to get us all killed. "Jerry!" I hiss again, gesturing for him to join me on the side of the building. "Get over here! Bring Tom!"

Ox stalks back from where he'd disappeared. "Get out of here!" he whisper-shouts.

Ignoring him, Tom whacks Jerry on the arm and points back inside. "Someone's in there. Who is it? Did they get a new plumber?"

Jerry whips toward the door and looks in, cupping his hands around his eyes. "They would *never*! Uh-oh."

My heart sinks as the door opens and the diner creep emerges, gun pointed right at Jerry as he backs him up. "Can I help you?" the creep growls.

Ox steps into view. "Stop! Police!"

Creepy dude looks toward Ox, and it's just enough time for Jerry, brave idiot that he is, to knock the gun out of the guy's hand. The guy takes off and Ox gives chase.

Further proving their idiocy, Tom and Jerry run inside.

I hear another set of screams from Mom and Goldie, and that's it. I run in after Tom and Jerry, only for them to skid to a stop in front of me.

"Move!" I shove them aside just in time to see Reid come barreling in from the back door.

"Freeze!" he yells.

The second guy, scary as all get out, sneers and points his gun at Reid. "I was wondering when you'd show up. Thought I might have to shoot someone."

"Drop your weapon," Reid says, his attention completely focused on the man.

He shrugs. "I don't think so. You see, the big boss is awfully pissed at you. Got the whole network looking for you. Said the first man to bring you down would get a hefty payday as thanks. So that's what we're doing here."

Reid scoffs. "Looks like a bunch of amateurs playing at being bad guys, if you ask me."

I'm stock still, watching the entire thing play out from my place right next to the counter. No one pays any attention to me as I inch closer. I can't see my family, but Goldie's whimpers haven't stopped. Behind me, Tom and Jerry have miraculously chosen to keep their mouths shut. I half wonder if they think this is all some big joke. A new kind of pre-breakfast entertainment.

Scary guy growls and steps toward Reid.

Without hesitating, Reid shoots him.

The man drops his gun and howls. "You shot my foot!"

Reid smirks. "That's how this works."

Out of nowhere, Thompson appears behind Reid and whacks him with his club. Reid crumples as my family shouts in surprise.

Thompson turns to them and *tsks*. "Honestly, this could have been handled so much better than this."

"A little help here?" the scary guy whines from his spot on the floor.

"Shut up," Thompson growls. "You've been a pain in my ass this whole time."

Goldie shrieks as Thompson starts to pull his gun out, and I've had enough. I grab Granny's skillet from its place of honor above the coffee pot and run through the swinging door, screaming like a banshee.

"You stop right there, you big meanie!"

Everything seems to dip into slow motion: Thompson turning toward me and clocking the way I'm raising the skillet into the air, scary dude scrambling to get out of my way, Reid lying motionless on the floor, Dad yelling for Thompson to drop the gun, and Thompson again, his eyes widening in a highly satisfying combination of fear and realization as I bring the skillet down on his head.

He drops like a lead balloon, the cast-iron skillet clanging onto his head a second time as it drops from my hands.

I know enough to look around for guns, to make sure none are close enough to Thompson or the scary guy to do any damage with. I don't see any.

"Are you okay?" I ask.

Mom and Goldie nod, while Dad just stares at me. I think he might be in shock.

I kneel beside Reid and feel for a pulse. It's there, and I exhale a sigh of relief.

"Willa?" Dad croaks. "Is that really you?"

Yeah. He's definitely in shock. I smile gently as I rise and grab a chef's knife, brandishing it in the most comforting way possible. "It's me, Dad. Turn around so I can cut the zip ties."

"Only you would use a giant knife when a pair of scissors would do the job just fine," Goldie manages to joke.

I ignore her while I position the business side of the knife at Dad's wrists. "Hold still," I mutter, then with one swipe of the knife, it's done.

I turn to Goldie, who's looking at me tearfully. "I'm so glad you rescued us," she says, the sobs coming again.

"Shh," I soothe, then gesture for her to swing around for me. I kneel behind her and cut the hard plastic.

Mom is next, and within seconds, all three are standing and hugging me, the chef's knife safely away from anyone.

"Everything okay back there?" Jerry's voice carries into the kitchen.

I roll my eyes. "*Now* you two pipe up?" I laugh.

Scary guy is still whimpering and bleeding at our feet, and there's no telling how long Reid and Thompson will be out. "Call 911," I instruct the duo. "We need an ambulance."

I COME TO with a start, jerking upright and feeling for my pistol.

"Easy, tiger," Willa says, smiling beside me.

That smile. *Christ.* I thought I'd never see it again. We're outside, and I'm on a stretcher. I relax, then wince. "My head."

"Yeah, Thompson really got you good," Willa says. "But don't worry, I gave him a taste of his own medicine."

"Yeah?" I greedily drink her in. "I love you."

Her face softens, then she smiles. "You sure that's not just the head wound talking?"

"No. I love you. I should have said something long before now. I think I've loved you from the second you yelled at me about the burger."

She laughs softly, and that's when I see the tears.

"Is everyone okay?"

She blows out a breath. "Mostly, yeah."

"Thompson," I start, then try to sit up. My head spins, but I push through the pain. "I'm going to kill him."

Willa smirks at me, then holds out a hand to help me sit

upright. "I don't think police officers are supposed to say things like that."

Once I get upright, I blink a few times, letting my vision clear. "Doesn't mean I still don't want to."

"Fair. The paramedics are working on the others." Then she gives me the rundown: Thompson and a guy that Ox chased down are in the back of the cruiser, and the guy Thompson shot is being treated en route to the hospital. Her family is shaken, but physically okay. Tom and Jerry, who caused the initial ruckus that launched everything into motion, are their usual rowdy selves and are probably already plotting how to make themselves look like the heroes in this whole thing.

"And you?" I look her in the eyes, searching for a sign.

She swallows. "You need your head checked."

My heart drops, but I let her hand me off to the paramedic. I squint at the guy. "You're new."

He smiles and pulls out his flashlight to check my eyes. "I've heard you're pretty new to town as well. I'm Aaron Joseph. My wife just got a job as the superintendent of schools down here, so here I am."

I nod. "You'll love it here."

He hums, then takes me through an examination. After he's done, he pulls his gloves off. "You've got a concussion; that's obvious. You could use a scan—"

"No." My reply is immediate and leaves no room for discussion.

Aaron laughs. "Yeah, I figured. It's mild. No working for a couple of days. Nothing physical. You know this drill, I suppose?"

"I do."

Ox reappears. "Thompson's responsible for everything."

I thank Aaron and join Ox on the sidewalk. Willa stands a bit away, talking with her family.

"That doesn't surprise me," I answer, "but I'm gonna need you to explain that."

"Turns out that Thompson is one of the Bunnies' informants." Ox's voice is deadly calm, and frankly, it's a little terrifying.

"Explain," I say again. "And give me a good reason for mysterious bruises not to end up on his face."

"Oh, you'll have to get in line for those, my friend." Ox's voice is just as calm as before. "Apparently, the Bunnies have people all over the coast that they keep on the payroll for any 'just in case' measures. When you got into town, Thompson tipped them off immediately."

"But how did he know who I was?"

Ox shrugs. "Lucky guess, I think. He didn't like the sound of you from the minute Chief said you were coming, and with you being from Miami? It's not hard to see how Thompson thought he'd be getting a solid payday for something related to you."

I shake my head, baffled. "What the hell was his plan? Especially today?"

Ox scoffs. "That idiot thought he'd be getting a million cash for turning you in. Best I can tell, without actually talking to him, is that he was going to take the money and skip town."

"How'd you get the intel if you didn't get it from him?"

"The guy I nabbed running out of the diner. Squealed like a piglet. Impressive, really—but I think he's hoping we'll put him somewhere the Bunnies can't get to him."

I snort. "Good luck with that."

Ox eyes me. "Agree. Anyway, did I hear the medic say you've got a concussion?"

I wave it off. "I'm fine. I know there's paperwork—"

"Get outta here with that shit," Ox says. "Go home, cuddle with your woman, and take a few days off. I've got it all under control."

"But—"

"No buts. It may seem like we're a small force, but there really *are* enough of us to handle this town without you. And Thompson. And Chief," he says with a wink. Then he leans forward. "Wanna see something?"

"Um, maybe?"

He gestures for me to walk with him. A few feet away sits the cruiser with Thompson in the back, and we walk up to it and look in. I give him a shit-eating grin when he looks my way.

He mouths a few choice words that start with F and sound a lot like "duck" and "ewe," but I just wave and grin a little wider.

"Being in the back is a good look for Thompson, don't you think?" Ox asks.

"Might be the best thing I've ever seen."

Willa approaches. "Let me take you home."

Twin feelings of hope and despair war within me. "It's okay. I can get myself home. Your family needs you."

She gives me a look. "Reid. I'm trying to take care of you. Let me do that."

I swallow hard. "I...okay."

I call my Miami chief to update him, but I keep the call brief, explaining I'll give full details later today or tomorrow. Then I look at Willa, who's staring at me and chewing on her nail. "Ready?"

She nods distractedly, then gestures down the street. "I parked down there."

We're quiet on the ride home. My head hurts, but my heart hurts worse. I told her I loved her, and she didn't say it back. Is this what she felt like when the roles were reversed?

It sucks.

When Willa finally gets us home after driving like a granny, she insists on me taking a shower and changing clothes. I want to argue with her about it, tell her that I'm perfectly fine, but the truth of it is, I'll do whatever she tells me to.

When I emerge from the shower in my favorite pair of gray sweatpants and a ratty tee, I find her sitting on my couch. Her eyes rake over me, and I allow myself to wonder what it would feel like to have this every day. What kind of miracle would it be to have Willa Dean Dash's love on a daily basis? To bask in it? To wake up to it, and endlessly work to be worthy of it? Of her?

"Reid," she starts.

But I shake my head and close the distance to her. "I need to say something first." I don't give her a chance to react before I'm on the couch beside her, pulling her hands to mine.

"I'm not leaving." I blurt the words out as fast as I can get them, and the way her eyes widen tells me that *maybe* I was a little intense with it. No matter. I keep going.

"I told you I loved you when I came to, and you didn't say it back. And that's okay—I don't want you to say it if you don't feel the same way."

"Reid—"

I hold a finger against her lips. "But I'm staying here anyway. I love this town. You're right. It's the best town ever. I feel more like myself here than I've ever felt at home, even though I don't know if I'll ever get over not being able to find really good Cuban food here. But that's not the point. The point is that I want this. I want us. I want you. I want to wake up and choose you every day. I want to earn your love every hour. I want to irritate the crap out of you with my insane food requests and say dirty things to you in public just to watch you blush. I want to flex my muscles and pop my dimples just to see you stumble, because it means I get to hold on to you and keep you from falling. I want all of you, and I'll wait as long as it takes, do whatever you need, for you to want me back."

Tears spring to her eyes. "I love you, too, you big oaf," she sniffs. "Sending you away was the dumbest thing I've ever done."

Midnight chooses this exact moment to yowl plaintively at our feet.

Willa laughs tearily. "Even Midnight agrees. She slept on your pillow last night and gave me nothing but grief this morning."

"So does this mean…" I trail off.

"I love you, Reid MacKinnon. I literally hit a man with Granny's skillet for you. If that doesn't say true love, what does?"

I stand and pull her up with me, wrapping my arms around her for a searing kiss. I'm never letting this woman go again.

CHAPTER 31

EPILOGUE

TEN MONTHS LATER

My gorgeous man stands at attention on the outdoor stage in the town square, his permanent Lucky Police Department badge glinting brightly in the afternoon sun. He's supposed to be paying attention to his uncle, but his eyes keep straying to me.

Watch! I mouth, hoping I come across as stern, but knowing I probably look more like an avenging cherub than anything. At least, that's what Reid tells me.

He winks and turns back to the ceremony.

Chief Mac is finishing a speech that is probably longer than it needs to be, but the man *is* retiring, so he can speak as long as he wants. Happily, he seems to be on the cusp of wrapping things up.

"And so it gives me the greatest pleasure to announce Lucky's next chief of police, Ox Hall!"

Everyone on the lawn claps and hollers. We had the vote earlier in the year, but this is the official handing-off of duty.

Ox, the big lug that he is, simply blinks back his emotions and steps forward to accept the badge that Chief Mac pins to his uniform. Then they shake, and Ox pulls the older man into a fierce embrace.

"Couldn't have happened to a better man," Matty says beside me, pocketing his cell after looking at it for the millionth time in the past hour.

"What's got you so glued to your phone?" I ask. "It's not calving season."

He purses his lips. "Nothing."

I sniff. "You know I know you're lying, right?"

"It's still not your business," he shoots back.

"Ooh, is it a girl?" I tease him. He says nothing, and I know I'm right. "When do I get to meet this mysterious woman?"

"Don't you have a diner to run?" he asks, clearly angling to change the subject.

I brighten. "I do!" Mom and Dad have agreed to let me buy the diner, but they're not quite ready to retire. They *are* ready for a three-month European vacation, though, and are flying out tomorrow. Which means yours truly is getting her first trial run at the place.

I squeal at the prospect and shake Matty. "It's mine! All mine!"

He laughs and extracts himself. "Yes, we know. We alllll know," he says as Goldie joins us, a camera strapped around her neck.

"About how excited she is to run the diner?" Goldie quips. "You'd think she's won the lottery."

"I basically have." And I mean it. I moved in with Reid about six months ago, and it's been amazing. He's full-time here in Lucky, and even brought all three of his parents up for us to meet. Agatha swears she's responsible for getting the two of us together and routinely cites the dinner Reid cooked as the moment love bloomed.

I don't have the heart to tell her otherwise, and neither does Reid. Which doesn't bode well for Goldie, since she's now in the little cottage behind Agatha's house and is next in line for "Agatha's Amorous Assignment," as Agatha keeps referring to it.

Yeah, it's hilariously weird. And I wouldn't have it any other way.

Reid catches my eye as he descends from the tiny stage, popping those delicious dimples and winking at me.

I wink back, even though it probably looks like butterflies are fighting on my face.

He grins wider as he nears. I'm happy to say that even though just about everything he does makes me weak in the knees, especially when he pairs it with a smoldering look that says he'd rather have one of us cuffed in the bedroom, I haven't fallen in the last month. Not literally, anyway.

Progress.

I jump into his arms when he reaches me, and he emits a grunt. "Nice to see you, too," he says around a kiss.

The click of a camera shutter goes off, and I pull myself away from my hunk of a man to see Goldie smiling mischievously at us. "Great photo," she grins. "Too bad Ox is front-page material, or you two would definitely be the news."

"I can't believe you're working for JJ," I groan, nestling into Reid's side as he squeezes me close.

"Someone has to take responsibility for moving the paper back to actual news," she says wryly. "Besides, as much as I love waiting tables, I don't want to do it for the rest of my life."

"Well, I, for one, am super proud of you," Matty says. "I think it's great you're the, what was it again?"

"Senior Photographer and Junior Staff Reporter," Goldie supplies.

I giggle. "Only JJ would come up with that as a title."

Goldie shrugs. "It works. Now I just have to convince him to pay for mileage when I travel outside Lucky's town limits."

Reid leans down to nuzzle my neck. "Wanna go home and let me see where *your* limits are?"

I hum, goosebumps flying across my body in response to his kiss. "Definitely."

We leave the town square, nodding our hellos to just about everyone we pass. Tom and Jerry sit on a bench to the side of the clock, and they wave as we pass. "See you tomorrow, Willa!" Tom calls.

Midnight greets us at the front door like always, yowling her displeasure at being left behind. She quiets when Reid produces a new toy from his pocket.

Reid turns to me. "You have far too many clothes on."

I gesture at him, still done up in full police gear, including the protective vest that he and Ox began insisting everyone on the force wear in the wake of the Bunnies business. "You're in more than me, Officer."

His forest-green eyes darken at the term, just like I knew they would, and he reaches around to swat my behind. "Naked. Now."

I reach around him and lock the door, smirking as I do so and beginning to back up. "And if I resist?"

He pulls his cuffs out, then undoes his utility belt and deposits it on the table in the front hallway. "Then I might have to punish you."

My blood heats. "Sounds promising."

Later, when we're lounging on the couch and deciding what to cook for dinner, it hits me all over again that this is my life. It's not perfect, but it's pretty close. "Hey, Reid?"

"Hmm?" He looks up from the menu-planning app he's been obsessed with lately.

"I love you."

The smile that breaks across his face sends my heart galloping. "I love you, too, Willa Dean Dash."

I lean over and kiss him. "Just Willa."

"I love you, too, Just Willa."

Also by Valerie Pepper

The Guided to Love Series

The Mechanic's Guide to Getting the Boss's Daughter (series starter novella)

The Widow's Guide to Second Chances (Book 1)

The Barista's Guide to The Perfect Steam (Book 2)

The Grump's Guide to Chaos (Book 3)

The Sacred River Series

Love Potion No. 69 (Novella, Book 1)

Karaoke Chemistry (Book 2)

The Lucky in Love Duology

Dining for Love (Book 1)

Dashing for Love (Book 2, Spring 2025)

Novellas

Naughty All The Way (November 2023) - Part of the Twelve Days of Smutmas limited-time collection

To Have and To Scold in the *Holidays & Hook-Ups* anthology by The New Romance Cafe (June 2023 - limited edition)

About the Author

Valerie Pepper is an incurable optimist and a firm believer in the girl getting the guy, or the guy getting the girl, or the girl getting the girl, or the guy getting the guy, or basically any way it needs to happen to make a real-life happily ever after, even if it takes more than one try.

When she's not writing, you can find her reading, walking, listening to whatever music suits her mood, and hanging out with her family. She's fascinated with the idea of a capsule wardrobe, but loves clothes and shoes and boots far too much to make a real go of it.

She's currently living out her own happily ever after in Birmingham, Alabama, with her family and maaaaaybe too many shoes. Learn more at www.authorvaleriepepper.com.

Acknowledgments

Thank you, as always, to my husband and kids. You don't read my smut, but you support and encourage me every day. Thank you for celebrating every milestone with me.

Thanks to my editor, Katie Awdas. Thank you to Melissa of Mel D. Designs for a beautiful cover.

Writing can be a solitary sport, but not when you have author friends like I do. To the Indie Chat and the Brat Pack: you're the best. Always.

Readers: Thank you, thank you, thank you. Thank you for the love you continue to show me and my books. Thank you for giving me your time, your enthusiasm, your memes, your exclamation points, grabby hands, hearts, and reviews. It means so much to me.

xo,